◈

To Lia —

In Solidarity —

Martínez

18 May 13

CHICANA & CHICANO VISIONS OF THE AMÉRICAS

The Block Captain's Daughter

Demetria Martínez

UNIVERSITY OF OKLAHOMA PRESS : NORMAN

This is a work of fiction. Names, characters, places, and incidents
are either the product of the author's imagination or are used
fictitiously, and any resemblance to actual events, locales,
or persons, living or dead, is entirely coincidental.

Library of Congress Cataloging-in-Publication Data
Martínez, Demetria, 1960–
The block captain's daughter / Demetria Martínez.
    p.   cm. — (Chicana & Chicano visions of the Américas ; v. 11)
ISBN 978-0-8061-4291-3 (pbk. : alk. paper)
I. Title.
PS3563.A7333337B57 2012
813'.54—dc23

                                        2011052844

The Block Captain's Daughter is Volume 11 in the
Chicana & Chicano Visions of the Américas series.

The paper in this book meets the guidelines for permanence and
durability of the Committee on Production Guidelines for Book
Longevity of the Council on Library Resources, Inc. ∞

1 2 3 4 5 6 7 8 9 10

In memory of Grace Paley

and

With gratitude to friends and mentors

Mimi López and Maria Teresa Marquez

The Block Captain's Daughter

❖

The Annunciation

———

Lupe

You can't believe the ninth month will ever arrive. But it will, and you know you'd better break the news without further delay.

Stretched out on the couch, watching a spider skittering across the ceiling, you say, "Precious one, the doctors took another picture yesterday. And it turns out . . . well, it turns out that you don't have a pee-pee after all. You, my love, are a girl."

Placing your hands on your belly, you wait for baby to stir. Nothing.

You go on. "Little one, all the time I took coming up with a name for you—Jesús Paul—was in vain. So I set about finding a replacement, no easy thing."

You look across the living room at the TV set and bite your lip. Every afternoon—after long days of waiting on tables at La Tropical—you watch infomercials to unwind. The one you enjoy the most features a doctor in a white coat advertising plastic surgery procedures. Face and butt, abs and boobs. Only in America, you think. No need to be embalmed at death when you can be embalmed throughout life. The doctor carries on for half an hour. Surgery can improve a woman's self-esteem, he crows. It can even change the course of her destiny.

"Now listen up, *mi preciosa*," you say, stroking your belly. "After much prayer I've decided that your name will be Destiny. Destiny Jane Anaya."

The baby kicks not once, not twice, but three times. You have no idea if the baby understands a word of what you've said. Still, you

———

worry. Thinking back to the names of your family in Mexico, you wonder if you've made a terrible mistake.

Adelina, Maudi, Encarnación, Consuelo, Lucinda, and Belén. There's even a Telesfora in there—a great-aunt who joined the Sisters of Loretto, where her name was changed to Crucita. The old-time names make you think of a cast-iron pot, unbreakable, with a lifetime guarantee. Destiny? For an instant it sounds light as cotton candy, too lightweight to pin the child to earth when she lands—a spirit no more, but a human being.

You feel around beside you in the folds of the couch and pull out your cell phone. You point it at the TV to turn it off—then catch yourself and reach for the remote on the coffee table. It has been this way for months—hormones scrambled, moods seesawing—leaving you unable to think clearly, especially at work where the gringos' orders have grown increasingly complex.

"Bean and cheese burrito, hold the cheese." "Huevos rancheros, egg whites only." "Tortillas, the kind without lard." "That's whole beans, please, not fried." Everyone's on one kind of diet or another. When you take orders you feel like a doctor scribbling out a prescription, life and death in your hands. What is the world coming to? The gringos believe in cholesterol the way Mexicanos believe in the existence of God. It's enough to make you ravenous.

You pull yourself up, go to the freezer, and take out two burritos, one for you and one for the child. Your mouth waters. You can just taste the trans-fatty acids.

"Hey Lupe, have a good one!" the mailman shouts through the screen door. *"Y tu también, Juan,"* you answer.

For three days you've let mail pile up: phone, electricity, and gas bills addressed to Guadalupe Gabriela Anaya. Some days you wish you could take a blade to those bills, cutting your name, so heavy with history, into confetti. Five hundred years ago Our Lady of Guadalupe appeared to a Nahuatl-speaking Indian. Two thousand years ago the angel Gabriel appeared to Mary. Visitations, annunciations. You understand such things all too well. Like Juan Diego and Mary, you had no choice but to say yes.

You crossed the Mexican border into Arizona on foot, the phone number of a cousin's cousin hidden in your bra, the sun a broken compass pointing you for days in all the wrong directions—forcing you, finally, to curl up beneath a Palo Verde tree to wait for death.

"Hey Lupe. It's Juan again. Somehow your *Time* magazine got in the wrong bundle. I'll add it to the rest of the stuff. Better take your mail in. Someone will think you're not home and break in."

"*Gracias,*" you say, opening the screen door. "It would be embarrassing, no? I was just elected Block Captain. I'm in charge of raising awareness about safety. My campaign platform was 'God helps those who help themselves.'"

You take the mail from the box as Juan moves on to the next house. Forgetting to lock your screen door, you return to your kitchen and set the burritos in the microwave. A few minutes later you take them, steaming, on a plate to a small round table covered with a lace tablecloth topped with a sheet of clear plastic. At the center of the table: a glazed, lime-green pitcher you spent a week's worth of tips on is filled to the brim with cold water.

After you curled up under the Palo Verde tree, you gripped your stomach to try to stop the cramping, which you feared was caused by drinking water out of a cattle trough. You fell asleep and dreamed of the things you'd seen on your journey: plastic water bottles scattered like headstones, empty sardine cans, a perfume bottle, toothbrush, toothpaste, a pocket Spanish-English dictionary, and a booklet of prayers to St. Anthony, finder of lost things.

When you woke up the stars shone like coins. They shone like the stars over China where the factory you had worked for relocated, leaving you and hundreds of women with no way to earn a living. Then one star fell so close you smelled it, then touched it. You put your finger in your mouth and savored: The star was made of lard, which you once spread on tortillas like it was butter, the main meal for you and your mother during the hard times. You pointed to the sky again and waited for another star to fall, but it did not. You thought of your mother. What will she do, you wondered, if I can't work and send money home? Even lard will be out of reach for her.

Phoenix is just around the bend, you said to the Palo Verde tree, only to realize no words had come out of your mouth. I will freshen up and apply for a job, you said, but again no words emerged. You closed your eyes and thought, I must be dead, and the words came out, sung sweetly in Chinese—your voice and those of hundreds of other women.

You made the sign of the cross and again fell asleep. You dreamed that your bones had turned to dust. In your dreams you heard the Palo Verde tree say, "Potential renal failure." And another tree answered, "Let's get her to the hospital in Tucson. Call the doctor from the church and have him meet us there." You dreamed you opened your eyes and saw a man and woman—your arms over their shoulders—walking you to a van.

"I'm Daniel," said the man, but you heard, Michael the Archangel. "I'm Shanti," said the woman, putting a wet rag on your forehead, as you rested your head on her lap. Like the man, she had fiery wings so large they hung out of the van's open windows. "We're from Southside Church," they said in unison, but you heard, Upon this rock you will build my church. "We're not going to turn you in to *la migra*," they said. But you heard, We were once strangers in the land of Egypt, therefore we must welcome the stranger.

◈

"Lupe, it's Cory."

"Come in, come in. I'm sitting here daydreaming while my burritos are getting cold. Let me thaw one out for you."

"Sounds good."

"They're bean, cheese, and red chile—nothing too hot. But I want this baby to get used to the red stuff now. Otherwise she'll grow up to be a ketchup Mexican. It happens to the best of us."

"Good news, Lupe. Virginia doesn't need her stroller any more. Don't worry about buying one."

You pull Cory's burrito out of the microwave and touch it to see if it is warm enough. Perfect. "*Gracias, chica,* but I don't need it. The neighbor gave me hers. One of those fancy ones the gringos use to run around the golf course with."

You open the refrigerator and reach in the back for the bottle of Taco Hell salsa, in case Cory wants to spice up her burrito.

Someday, you think, you might tell Cory the truth. That you dipped into your savings and bought the stroller brand-new from KMart. That one of the things you saw in the desert was a stroller, abandoned by a mother and her child whose fate you can only imagine. Your baby will have a different destiny.

"Okay, Cory. Don't forget our vow. We're going to speak only Spanish for an hour every week. You're coming along so well."

"Ay, Lupe, how would I make it without you?"

"You'd make it just fine."

You fetch two glasses and the green pitcher, imagining that it is filled with wine that some miracle worker turned into water, clean and cool for you and Cory to drink as you lead her, word by word, into the Spanish language.

◆

My Dearest Destiny,

What a strange thing it is to take on this letter, seeing as how my waters have yet to part that you might cross into our humble promised land of Albuquerque, New Mexico. Warnings first. I am terrible at talking on paper. Out loud I am good, for the life of the poor foreigner depends upon speech. In this land one must explain, explain, explain—to doctors, bank tellers, and bosses—lest they inject you with the wrong medicine or count your money out wrongly or order extra work for no extra pay. I have learned to line up my words as in a Scrabble game that I might score high and emerge alive. So it shall be for you, who are already ahead of the game.

Nowadays all the experts say that prenatal readings make for Ivy League–bound babies. So nightly I grit my teeth and read to you from the best-selling Harry Potter book. I can only hope to God that my womb is equipped with good speakers, that my efforts to smarten you up come to something. I am no fan of Harry Potter, preferring to read murder mysteries before nightly prayers. Oh well. When the doctor yanks you into the light of day and slaps you on the behind, may you cry out, Harry! Harry!

Let me say that writing to you is not my bright idea. I do so under orders from my dearest friends, Maritza, Flor, Cory, and Peter. Posterity! Posterity! I learned this word in their hounding me to do this. I considered and prayed. And it came to me that one day I will be sitting in my lawn chair on the porch with a weak mind and not much going on but swatting flies and cracking walnuts with the friends listed above. I might forget my own story. So it is that I am writing you this letter, with more to come, *Si Dios quiere*. I have decided to say yes to posterity.

Love,

Your Mama,
Guadalupe Gabriela Anaya,
Block Captain of Sunflower
Street SE

What Saves Us

———

Peter

On our second date, we ponder the mysteries of insulin. "Just think," Cory says. "When you add beans to your meal, sugar digests slowly and moves safely into the bloodstream over a period of four to six hours."

She lifts the lid of her Crock Pot and salts the beans. She asks me to clear the kitchen table. It's piled high with obscure monographs detailing the effects of traditional indigenous fare on blood sugar imbalances, such as diabetes.

"Tepary beans, nopalitos, mesquite flour, prickly pear nectar, chia seeds," says Cory. "Chicano and Native American test subjects who have added these ancient staples to their diets are reporting remarkable improvements."

She leans back against the sink, arms crossed, and smiles.

"It explains everything, Peter," she says.

"Yes," I say, clueless.

She goes on as she sets out the silverware. "Every night now when I watch the news I see evidence that blood sugar levels of wealthy white males are fluctuating—and causing everything. Road rage. Refusal to fund after-school programs for children. Union busting and impulse bombing abroad."

"You're on to something, Cory, no doubt about it."

Now, I am of the opinion that capitalism run amok is at the root of all evil, but I have to show my solidarity with her, which I hope she'll find sexy. On our first date at El Patio I was so nervous I couldn't stop talking about Venezuela's offer to supply poor

———

Americans with gasoline at a discount. By 8 p.m. Cory said she was tired. I walked her back to her apartment on Columbia Street, and we said good night at the gate.

I was surprised when, a week later, she asked me to her place for a meal. Which was a good thing. Because by the time we had made it through our second round of Corona beer at El Patio, I'd made up my mind that I wanted to marry her.

I'll admit it. I'm the marrying kind. Twice I goofed up. I married women too young for me, both red-headed Irish gals who didn't know the basics. Like the fact that the North American Free Trade Agreement has pushed millions of Mexicans off their lands, forcing them to come north to find work. Facts that sometimes keep me up at night, having imaginary arguments with anti-immigrant racists.

Cory's different from those other women. She knows a thing or two. Like how to cut a man open in three places: through the skull, the wrist, and the torso. Now you might wonder what Japanese sword fighting has to do with free trade. I'm not so sure myself, but suffice it to say that when she used Japanese words to describe the lethal dance that is Kendo, my heart quivered. "I've devoted my life to the sword," she said solemnly, running her hands through her short brown hair.

❖

"Supper's just about ready," she says, flipping tortillas over the gas flame. "I hope you don't mind. I got these low-carbohydrate things. I'll blacken them a bit so they don't taste like cardboard. I'm trying to lose five pounds."

Most women don't realize they can lose five pounds in an instant just by standing up straight. Cory's at that age, in her mid-thirties, when women start to slump and cross their arms, as if apologizing for taking up too much space in a man's world. That's how I see it anyway. My mom was a big woman and not afraid to express herself. When my dad got drunk and beat her up, it was like he was trying to beat her back down to size again.

"You look good just the way you are." If only she could see what I see—a body with curves in all the right places, and rich olive skin that she doesn't cover up with makeup—which invariably goes orange on Chicana skin.

We sit down to our feast. I pause before picking up my spoon in case she believes in prayers before meals. Evidently not. She takes shredded cheese and rolls it in a corn tortilla like she's rolling a cigarette.

"So tell me, Peter. What brought you to New Mexico?"

I can hear in her voice that this is a test. I don't know a single native New Mexican who delights in the arrival of newcomers, especially those with money. I will have to set myself apart by telling her the truth.

"I confess, Cory, I'm a cliché. I moved to Santa Fe to start life over. To do what I couldn't get away with in my own hometown. Cocaine. Classes in shamanism. I had an affair with a married woman and justified it by saying I was tying up loose ends from a past life."

Cory puts her spoon down and laughs. Her dimples appear, and it takes everything for me not to reach out and rub my hand along her cheek. She laughs so hard tears squeeze out of her eyes. Strangely enough, I don't feel laughed at, so much as forgiven.

"I moved to Albuquerque when my money ran out, and luckily I found work translating documents for various businesses. I was able to subsidize my activism—translating for human rights delegations here and in Latin America."

"Nice," Cory says. She plucks her paper napkin from her lap and slowly tears it in two. She gets up to stir the beans, even though the Crock-Pot is turned off. "Lucky you," she says quietly. Something in her voice, so full of sunlight, has changed, as if a cloud has passed over it. "There's plenty of food," she says, as if I can't see the feast spread out before us.

"Yes, I am lucky. My mother was a high school Spanish teacher. When she died I inherited her car. The first time I used it, a week or so after the funeral, the radio blasted on—set to the local Spanish station. And I realized I'd lived all my life on the opposite end of the dial from my mother—National Public Radio, rock, rap. I signed up for a Spanish class at the community college the next day."

It's not a whole lot to expect someone to say "I'm sorry" upon hearing of the death of a parent, even if it's old news. Instead, Cory fiddles with her bottle of beer then pours an inch more into her glass. I feel like I'm at my Sunday Quaker meeting, but there's nothing blessed about this silence. I want nothing more than to apologize—to get on with this wonderful evening I hope will end with a kiss—but Cory has yet to name the sin of which I'm guilty. It's not fair.

"My father is not bilingual. But when he's sober, he's articulate. He's good at things English is good at, like threatening to sue. He's an attorney. I haven't spoken to him in years."

Cory says nothing so I go on. "He's a get-to-the-point kind of person. Not one to talk in rough draft, if you know what I mean. Not one to be vulnerable."

"More beer?" Cory asks.

"No," I say, imagining walking out of the apartment and slamming the door behind me. "On second thought, yes," I say, wondering if one day she will be my wife. Some Quaker I am. They make all decisions by consensus, and here I am of two minds, irreconcilable.

She pours the rest of the beer into my glass as I panic over what to say that will yank her out of her netherworld. Then Mother Nature comes to the rescue. We hear the slamming of the screen door and tapping on the picture window. It's hail popping off the glass. Wind bends the branches of the locust tree in the courtyard of the apartment complex.

"Moisture!" Cory shouts. "Maybe the drought won't be as bad as it was last year." I follow her to the other end of the room, where we kneel like children on the couch and face the window. A minute later a rainbow appears amid shards of sunlight. When the rainbow disappears we sink down into the couch.

"Check these out," Cory says, wiping dust from some books arrayed on her coffee table. "They're from the used bookstore, Birdsong. When I'm in a funk I go there. The aroma of old paperbacks alone makes me forget why I'm feeling so bad."

I look through the stack. All the books are about New Mexico history and include Fray Angelico's research on New Mexico families. "I take it your people have been here for a while," I say.

"My great-great-great-great grandparents lived in what was then New Spain—which would later become Mexico, then a U.S. territory and then the U S of A. We've been on this land for centuries. And when you take into account that we're mestizos, descendants not only of Hispanos but Native Americans—well, the indigenous origin stories tell us we've been here since the beginning of time."

I have a feeling Cory's done this a lot, ticking off her genealogy to impress men like me. That's the thing with these New Mexico women. They can make you feel like a lightweight, with no history to pin you to the earth. They can drive you crazy with desire, too. I imagine making love to her. I picture her on top of me, her weight holding me down, bringing an end to my wanderings, my loneliness. Cory, who can cut a man to pieces in three places, may be my only hope.

Then she asks the dreaded question. "Where are your people from?"

I pick up Fray Angelico's book, go to the footnotes and clear my throat. "I never bothered to find out," I lie. "I've no idea where they're from."

One of the footnotes, circled in red ink, refers to records kept by the Catholic Church during the Spanish Inquisition. Why can't I tell Cory the truth? That I have spent years trying to find out where my people are from but the woman who gave me up for adoption asked that no information ever be given out to me, her son. Long ago I forgave her for choosing not to raise me. But I can never forgive her for denying me a family tree—the names, dates, and places that might endow me—just another white guy—with a history.

I stare down at the page. "I've never met a footnote I didn't like," I say with a chuckle. "My major in college was history."

I want Cory to believe that a raindrop has plopped on the page, but she knows better. She pulls up close to me and puts her hand on my back as I wipe my eyes with my sleeve.

"Peter. What's wrong?"

"Jeez, this stuff comes up when I least expect it. Some dinner guest I am."

"It's alright. What's up?" She takes my hand in hers.

I tell her about my fruitless search to find my biological mother.

Cory searches my face with her pitch black eyes. "It never occurred to me," she says. "It's easy to assume things. Those of us from old New Mexico families can be, well, haughty about the fact of our roots. I'm really sorry."

"You did nothing wrong. These are my issues. But I would like to know something. What did I say during dinner that pissed you off?"

"It was that obvious, huh?"

Cory leans forward, her elbows propped on her knees. "Your story. It's the same old thing. People like you with enough money to reinvent themselves in Santa Fe. The old timers pushed out because of jacked up property taxes. It's just the shits when—."

"You mean white people. That's what you're saying, right? Go back where we came from, even if we don't know where we came from."

"Peter, that's not what I meant. Hear me out. Forget what I said. I'm not pissed off at you. It's me I'm pissed off at. You have what I've wanted more than anything in my life. Spanish. I blew my one big chance to learn Spanish."

Now it's Cory who's fighting back tears. I'm happy. For a moment I can hurt her as much as she hurt me.

"I went to Stanford intending to major in Spanish. Instead I majored in depression. That was before I dropped out."

We sit in silence for a long time. The sun is setting. Gold light saturates the living room wall where a wooden sword hangs on hooks.

"Cory, is that the sword you use in Kendo?"

"Yes, one of them. It's a *bokken*. We use it to practice different stances."

She gets up to get it, then spreads the heavy blunt sword across our laps.

"Beautiful, huh?"

"Why did you take up Kendo?"

"I wanted a man—the student teacher—to notice me. That was in my twenties." She smiles and shakes her head.

"But the reason I stick with it—that's important. When you're up against someone, you keep the tip of the sword aimed at your opponent's throat. One hundredth of an inch off center and you're done for. You've left an opening. Of course you're always wearing a mask, but in essence, you have bared your throat."

She runs her hand over the sword. "In the most difficult moments of life I remember to seek the center. I don't know what that means. But I think it has saved me."

She returns the sword to its place on the wall and joins me again on the couch.

"It's clear outside," I say. "How about a walk?"

She closes the Fray Angelico book then looks at me. "It's all going to be okay, you know."

"Yes," I say, not knowing what she means and not needing to know. "Come on, let's go outside. I love the smell of rain."

In Love, In War

Maritza

Vats of salsa are steaming at the Frontier Restaurant and I'm in line, eager to ladle the hot stuff onto my Western omelet, when I hear his voice, "Hey Maritza." I see it's Adam Guest, a handsome blonde man who asked me out on a date one night—dinner here at the Frontier.

"*Como estás?*" Adam asks.

"*Muy bien, gracias a Dios,*" I say, using the respectful answer where you give God the credit for having had the good luck to live to see another day.

"*Y tú? "Cómo has estado?*"

"*Muy bien,*" he responds.

Now you have to understand: Adam doesn't speak a word of Spanish. No, I take that back. He speaks six words if we count charitably and add "Hola Maritza" to his repertoire—which is fine by me. I can afford to be generous. I've got a way with numbers. I keep the books for the Albuquerque Peace and Justice Center, and neither God nor luck has kept us in the black for three years in a row.

I'm one of those endangered species— a person who loves writing grants. Rows of numbers look like wood columns to me, ramadas holding up the sky under which believers in justice and peace can dream their dreams and hammer out their strategies. Deadlines? There is nothing as exhilarating as an online application due at any moment; nothing like staring at a computer screen as if through a windshield after a car wreck. I know how to resuscitate language, to describe the New Mexico no one wants to see, the birthplace and testing fields of the atomic bomb. Fiscal year by fiscal year I've managed to convince funders that the Land of Enchantment is the belly of the beast, and what the Peace Center does has ramifications nationwide.

"How on earth do you manage to pull all those funds in?" Adam had asked me, hiking his eyebrows in wonder, on what would be our first and last date.

"Easy. I use Chicana-style fundraising."

"How does that work?"

I pointed my hand in the shape of a pistol and aimed it at him. "Stick 'em up," I said.

He smiled and blushed. I'd said the magic word. Chicana. Daughter of the Mesoamerican holocaust of 500 years ago. Survivor of America's theft of these lands starting some 150 years ago. Just the kind of woman who can provoke guilt in good men, like Adam.

"So what barrio did you grow up in?"

"My family lived near the University of New Mexico law school, and the golf course. Dad taught at the law school."

"But that neighborhood must have been all white."

"Yes, until we single-handedly integrated it."

"You must have encountered a lot of racism."

"The cops stopped Dad all the time and questioned him when he'd go out for a walk. Then he started carrying around a golf club. They mistook him for a golfer."

"But he shouldn't have had to do that."

"Yeah, well, it turns out he took up golf after he had a heart attack. Doctor's orders."

"I was lucky," I continued. "My parents are middle class. I had a happy childhood." Adam put his fork down in a lake of salsa. He leaned back in the booth. I imagined the color draining from my face; brown as I am, he was seeing white. But before the spell was entirely broken, I managed to talk him into setting out chairs at the next People Before Profits film night at the Peace Center.

Now a good friend, Adam waited with me while his food was being prepared. The number 92 appeared on a digital screen. "There's my number," Adam says. "I'd better get my food while it's hot."

"Say, Adam, you haven't seen Flor, have you?"

"I saw her in the parking lot getting out of her truck."

"Good. I've been looking for her. Go enjoy your meal. *Hasta luego.*"

My food drowning in salsa, I make my way through the crowd into the middle room and grab a booth beneath a painting, one of dozens, of John Wayne. No sign of Flor yet. Wearing her signature jeans, turtle necks, and ostrich skin boots, she's hard to miss. She has hair that hangs below her waist. Her hair has such a sheen to it that when she shakes her head it looks like it's reflecting lightning. I swear the first time we made love I could see myself reflected in that hair; it was like walking into a hall of mirrors, but instead of seeing your body as a series of distortions, you see only beauty. I'd never seen my body that way before. A lot of women, when around an attractive man, hold their stomachs in, however slightly. With Flor Hinojosa Shapiro, I exhaled completely, maybe for the first time in my adult life.

"*Preciosa*, sorry I'm late," she says, slipping into the seat across from me. "I went on a run and lost track of time."

Her hair is tied back in a braid and pinned up. She's got sweats on and running shoes, size six. When we're at home and she takes her shoes off I can't imagine how those feet, so small, anchor her to the earth. Maybe they're not supposed to. She's Jewish. Her great-grandparents fled pogroms in Russia; her grandparents fled Hitler's Germany for Cuba. Her parents ended up in Albuquerque. If you're one of the Chosen People, God will part the Red Sea for you time and again, but you'd better be good at running since you don't know how long the walls of water will hold.

"I'm going to have to get over to the prayer vigil. They need a Spanish speaker," Flor says. "Univisión wants an interview with me." Flor organizes weekly vigils for Stop the War Machine.

"You've got a long evening ahead of you. Here's an extra fork. Dig in."

"Just a few bites, then I'm off to change into some decent clothes. My blazer and skirt are stashed at the Peace Center."

I touch my lips, then her cheekbones, coating them lightly with red lipstick.

"There you are, camera ready. You look great."

No matter what Flor is wearing, she manages to look good. Put her in front of a camera and she looks even better. She's like a plant; keep her away from the light for too long and she wilts. In front of the blazing lights of television cameras, her face blossoms as she cites statistics about the numbers of soldiers and civilians dead in Iraq and Afghanistan, her dimpled olive face, in all its glory, filling the entire screen.

"Good news," she says. "The archbishop, a rabbi, and an imam have all confirmed that they will join us next week and make statements to the press. It's been a great day."

She would never admit this, but every day has been a great day for her thanks to George W. Bush. Her anti-war work has been good for her. She went from taking fifty milligrams of an anti-depressant before Bush invaded Baghdad to twenty-five milligrams right after the invasion when she got involved with the vigils. She halved her pill again and again until she crossed over into that mysterious mathematical zone of infinite divisions invisible to the eye. In the midst of all this death, Flor got her life force back.

"Come with me to the vigil," she says, scooping eggs into her tortilla.

"Thanks, but you go do your thing. I'll wait for you at home. It's been a long day."

"And you want nothing more," she says with a grin, "than to climb into bed with your stash of porn."

"Okay, I confess. Instead of holding a sign, I'd rather read my Ladies Home Journal and Good Housekeeping."

"Whatever floats your boat, honey. When you read of a new use for apple cider vinegar and baking soda you get a look of peace that passeth all understanding," she says, paraphrasing scripture. "At least my understanding."

She playfully taps my leg with her foot beneath the table.

"Hey, I'll bet you don't know that to untangle a fine jewelry chain, rubbing it with oil first does the trick. Or that the Intrepid vacuum cleaner we were thinking of buying has been recalled. It's been discovered that its rotors are locking and overheating, creating a fire hazard."

Almost every day while listening to National Public Radio on KUNM, I clip and glue these kinds of tips and warnings onto index cards then file them carefully by topic.

Even my buddy Rubén, who got me a subscription to Good Housekeeping for my birthday, likes to rib me about my reading habits. "What happened to the good old days," he teases, "when you majored in women's studies and called me up to read passages from *When God Was a Woman*?"

What he and maybe even Flor don't understand is that more than ever, I believe God is a woman. She is Demeter, Tonantzin—grain goddesses both, archetypes of plenty and the well-tended home—the opposite of the Iraq I hear about on the radio, where bombed houses, beyond repair, look like shadowy skulls.

"Come on," I tell Flor, "let me walk you to the parking lot."

"No need, love. Stay here and finish your meal. I'll see you tonight after the vigil."

❖

"Shock . . . Awe . . . here kitty, kitty!" Two cats with paws that look like cotton balls swarm around my ankles as I unlock the door to the adobe house I share with Flor. The cats' real names are Scratch and Sniff, but Flor changed them after Bush spoke of Shock and Awe to describe his method of bombing. The cats will get their real names back after the war is over, Flor told me back when we began dating. "In the meantime," she said, "they're constant reminders of what we're up against."

I still can't imagine why Flor would need more reminders than she already has: three television sets—one in the living room, one beside the kitchen sink, and another in the bedroom—all tuned to news stations, the sound muted. Like much of the rest of the world, she had the news on 24/7 when the Twin Towers fell on 9/11. "I've never bothered to turn the news off," she explained. "Might as well keep it on. Something else might happen."

After feeding the cats, I get into my pajamas and slippers then put on water for tea. The long wood counter dividing kitchen from living room is piled high with Flor's manila folders, all filled with information for her dissertation. She's writing about the faith-based Sanctuary Movement of the 1980s, when US citizens clandestinely aided refugees who'd fled U.S.–backed dictatorships in Central America. Funny the way Flor claims she's not religious or even spiritual. I've never met anyone so preoccupied by questions of good and evil. She's the granddaughter of a Holocaust survivor. The question that haunted her grandmother and her parents was how so many Germans could look the other way as Jews were carted off to death camps. Flor's question is what makes some people not look the other way, as in the case of the Sanctuary Movement, and instead conspire against their government with the intent to save lives.

Steam swirls upward as I lift the slow cooker lid to spread the aroma of Cuban-style black beans throughout the house. The beans have been cooking all day with onions, bell peppers, tomatoes, cumin, garlic, and more. It smells divine. Next to the slow cooker is the coffee maker, its red light still on from this morning. Clicking it off I remember with a smile the night Flor had me over for the first time. I sat down on her couch while she loaded up her grandmother's silver antique tray with flan, Cuban rum, and two mugs of coffee.

I took long sips of the coffee. Alcohol has never lessened my inhibitions, but caffeine is another story: halfway into a cup and my blood runs hot. My temples began to throb as I took in Flor's hazel eyes. Then she looked boldly at my chest. "Great T-shirt," she remarked, "We're Making Enemies Faster Than We Can Kill Them." Her hand slid slowly toward mine. I was about to touch it when she said, "I hope the coffee is okay. It's decaf. I can't drink caffeine at night and sleep."

Seduction by placebo, I thought, disbelieving. I panicked. But the feeling dissipated as Flor reached for my face, drew me close, and kissed me. After a while, we moved to her bedroom. For the first time in my life I made love with a woman. Flor, a beautiful flower, stretched out beside me in bed.

The next day I called Rubén and asked him how I should break the news to my father. "Just tell it like it is," he advised. "It's not like you just up and decided to become a lesbian. There's a war on. Flor chairs the vigil committee at the Peace Center. You keep the place solvent. She starts asking you out."

I forgot Rubén's script when I stopped by my father's house. "Dad, do you have a minute?" He was on the couch reading *The New York Times*. "I have ten minutes," he said. "Then I go get the results of my biopsy. Prostate. Remember?"

"I have something to tell you. I hope you won't be upset."

"I'm pondering my mortality. It concentrates the mind, as they say."

"I'm dating a lesbian, dad." He carefully dog-eared the editorial page before setting the paper down beside him. He ran his fingers through his non-existent hair.

"Doesn't that make you one? A lesbian?" he asked, his brows furrowed.

"Well, I, I . . ."

He glanced at his watch. "Does she come from good family, *buena gente*? In our culture that's what matters—don't ever forget it."

"Her parents are professors. They're Cuban."

"Do they see through George Bush's dirty tricks?"

"Yes."

"Well, you could do worse."

"So you're not upset?"

"*Mijita*, all I know is that I want mariachis to perform at my funeral."

Dad still calls me "*mijita*," my little girl.

Tears started streaming down my face. "I still have to tell Mom."

Dad handed me five dollars. "Here, go treat yourself to one of those fancy coffees at Winnings. I'll tell your mom."

The phone rings as I pour hot water over chamomile buds, remembering Dad's elation when he told me the doctors gave him a clean bill of health. It's Flor calling to let me know she's on her way. Soon I hear her truck tires crunching on the gravel as she drives up to the house.

"*Amor*, will you give me a hand?" she asks as she steps into the house. "I need help carrying something in."

"What is it?

"A surprise. An early Christmas gift for both of us to enjoy."

I rub my hands together. "Sounds like we're in for some fun." I've told Flor for some time that I want a record player for Christmas. My old one gave out, but I've saved all my vinyl records. What I miss most are my albums of mariachi music that Dad gave me over the years for my birthday.

We go out to the truck. Between the two of us we manage to carry a bulky box into the house and set it on the couch.

"Here love, you open it," Flor says, handing me a pair of scissors.

I slit the box and tear off the panels of cardboard.

"Merry Christmas!" Flor hollers.

It's a television set. The screen is black and shiny as polished granite. It makes me think of the Vietnam Veterans Memorial in Washington, DC.

"The TV in the bedroom is about to give out. Last night while you were gone I was watching a program about soldier suicides, and the screen went static for ten minutes."

Flor runs her hand over the top of the television set. She smiles, her face glowing. I half expect her to break into song. She pulls the instruction booklet from the cardboard. She turns the pages reverently. I can hardly believe what I'm seeing.

"I'm sure it was a very informative program, Flor. Now give me a hand. We're putting this thing back in the truck, and either you or I will return it to the store tomorrow."

"What?"

"I'm tired of you having to watch the news before we make love. Not only that but I can't stand the way the TV light flickers when we do make love. I feel like a cop car with its lights on is pulling up behind me."

When Flor finally finds her voice she booms: "And you don't think I'm tired of the damn war? You know that I agreed to monitor local and national news for Stop the War Machine. You've known this since we first started dating."

"But twenty-four hours a day? We can watch the news in the living room like civilized people. I'm sorry but we don't need a TV in the bedroom."

"You don't get it, do you, Maritza? I keep the news stations on because—."

"Because something might happen. I know, I know. I've heard that a million times from you. But you know what, Flor? We've been together now for God knows how long. And guess what? Almost nothing happens. The rich slaughter the weak then lie about it. That's it."

Flor's crying now. Rivulets of mascara are running down her rouged, camera-ready face. This is no longer the dimpled face that fills the TV screen. It's an old and tired and sad face. It's her grandmother's face, the grandmother who survived the Holocaust. The woman whose picture hangs in our bedroom. A woman who knew all too well that things do happen. Unthinkable things that happen with so little warning not even God can react in time to save his people.

I try to put my arms around Flor, but she turns away and grabs the keys to her truck. Behind her the living room screen lights up. Univisión is doing a special report on Baghdad, using footage of the U.S. invasion. The light from the bombing is as bright as that of a bonfire. Flames lick the TV screen. I half expect them to leap out of the television set. Normally, Flor would be on the couch, riveted by the scenes of destruction, her worst fears about humankind confirmed.

She drops the key, grabs the remote from the coffee table and points it at the TV. "Let's just turn this off for good," she says, but I snatch the device from her hand.

Suddenly Univisión cuts to the vigil. I turn the sound on. There's

Flor in front of a large gathering of people, their faces awash in candlelight. In flawless Spanish she explains that representatives of a dozen organizations are present to bear witness to the madness of war and to demand a withdrawal of all U.S. troops from Iraq. I feel like I'm seeing a woman entirely different from the one who stands beside me. The one haloed in camera light believes, if only for a moment, that if enough people tire of war and destruction, the world might not go up in flames, after all.

I reach for Flor's hand. We sit down on the couch. She stares at her image. She's like a child who is seeing herself for the first time in a mirror. She turns to me, her eyes now pleading. "I'm doing everything in my power to change the story," she says, waving at the TV screen, filled again with scenes of bombing. "To make the ending come out differently." She cries some more.

"I know, honey, I know," I say, wiping away my own tears. "That's why I'm here for you. I want a different ending, too."

The next day after Flor leaves for the university library, I manage to get the new television set into the bedroom. I stare at the blank screen for a long time then turn the set on. To my surprise, Univisión is rerunning footage from last night's vigil. The phone number for the Peace Center is running at the bottom of the screen. I don't know how the story will end but no matter what, I have to keep my vow to Flor. I go to the bathroom to wash my face and put on my makeup so that I can get to work.

◈

My Dearest Destiny,

In anticipation of the Big Day, I have tossed and turned and prayed over this question: Who shall I choose to be Destiny's godparents? Brace yourself. For your Mama has selected four persons, each examples of holiness, which will serve you well in this vale of tears. I speak of Maritza, Flor, Cory, and Peter.

Maritza, still a church-goer, will drive you to Mass each Sunday should I become incapacitated in body or in mind, in keeping with the catechism.

Flor? She's Jewish, this I know, but Jesus was too, so no contradictions there. She will teach you to pray Friday night Sabbath prayers in Hebrew, and thus you shall honor your ancestors, many of whom practiced Judaism in secret during the dreadful times of the Inquisition.

Peter? He's a Quaker. Should you ever convert to another path, it would not break my heart to see you go the way of the Quakers. Peter took me to one of their worship services. Unlike Catholics they sit in silence, contemplating Our Lord, not wasting His time worrying over what He said about women priests, gayness, birth control, and the like. So if you find God in all that silence, you shall hear no protest from me.

Cory? Now this took some thinking. She's tending toward Buddhism but might revert to being an agnostic, neither believing nor disbelieving, whatever that means. But such children of God, atheists included, are on this earth to keep the rest of us humble. After all, nobody has produced a photograph of God. There is no proof that He exists, so in these end times we go by blind faith. We will know nothing for sure until we die and encounter Him in all his Glory and not only that—uh oh, my lunch break is almost up and I see Mr. Simmons, our vengeful boss, pointing at his watch. One last thing: You should be proud of your Mama, who last night gave a speech at the Block Captain's meeting about keeping the television on when leaving home, full blast, so as to give impressions that someone is always at home, thus deterring thieves. Your Mama has missions to accomplish in this our world, and so she does her best, house by house, neighbor by neighbor and with great fervor . . . oh no, lunch time is up. *Ya me voy.*

Love,

Mama

What the Heart Says

Cory

You wake up one morning to discover that you can roll your *R*s. You say your name, *Socorro, Socorro,* as you gaze in the mirror like a girl testing her mother's lipstick on the sly. You open the curtain to let in more light, then glance around the room. Towels, *toallas.* Bathtub, *bañero.* Window, *ventana.* Two-by-two the words come at you, creatures paired miraculously as in Noah's ark. Soap, *jabon.* Shower, *ducha.* Mirror, *espejo. Gracias a Dios,* you whisper, thanks be to God.

But come to think of it, God has nothing to do with this gift of tongues.

❖

"Enough bitching about not speaking Spanish, Cory," says your husband Peter, an Anglo fluent in four languages. He sits down at the computer. "I'm going online."

A day later a package arrives: flash cards for Latinos who grew up hearing the language but not speaking it; the tongue-tied who ace classes but can't ask for directions to the nearest Laundromat; the guilt-ridden for whom Spanish is a pre-existing condition that flares up when ordering food at a Mexican restaurant, then recedes when the margaritas wear off.

For a week the package sits unopened in its brown wrapping on the piano. You look at it, embarrassed, as if it were a sex toy.

"Come on, open it," says Peter.

"Stop telling me how to run my life," you answer, heading to the

---

backyard hammock to watch the sunset. Why did I marry that man, you wonder, flicking a mosquito off your wrist. What did I see in him the night he stood up at the Quaker Meeting House to debut his film about union activists in Oaxaca? Peter, with his goofy ponytail barely rooted to his balding head, sporting a Guatemalan peasant shirt and $125 sandals made of recycled tires. Still, you had to admit the film was brilliant and, thankfully for you, it had English subtitles. And ever since then, you have felt like Peter's English subtitle.

After the sun sets behind the west mesa, you return to the house. Peter has left a note, saying he's at a meeting. You stare at the flash card package. "This is no way to live," you say, box cutter in hand. You slit the box open. You spread the cards on the kitchen table as if to read the tarot, terrified of false promises of fluency. A statue of St. Anthony, finder of all that is lost, looks on as you read each word then flip the card over. Stars, *estrellas*. Flames, *llamas*. Stones, *piedras*. The hours pass. You stretch out on the couch and doze. You dream of summers with your bilingual grandma—how English went in your one ear, Spanish in the other, mellowing inside you, a beautiful *mole* of sound.

You wake up and return to your game of linguistic solitaire. At midnight Peter comes home and smells the burnt black beans you'd left simmering. You're asleep at the table, your head cradled in your arms. Saying nothing, Peter makes you an omelet. Gently, he shrugs you awake and hands you a fork. Next to St. Anthony he sets up a small TV he's rescued from the garage so that you can watch *telenovelas* or hear the rosary recited in Spanish on the Catholic station. He kisses you on the head, then leaves for Brazil.

❖

Night, *la noche*, turns into day, *el dia*. Summer, *el verano*, turns into fall, *el otoño*.

The kitchen table, meanwhile, becomes a country all its own, with Spanish-language newspapers from around the world: grammar books your friend Maritza brought you and CDs of Cuban music—with printed lyrics—that Flor dropped off. Lupe drills you on common mistakes new Spanish speakers make, so that you will not say you are *embarasada*, pregnant, when you mean to say you are embarrassed.

Things begin to happen. When you go for your mammogram, a nurse runs out to the lobby, asking if anyone speaks Spanish. You follow her to a small office. A Mexican woman has misunderstood the doctor's words; she thinks she has cancer. You take the chart from the nurse, sit beside the woman and hold her hand. You deliver the happy news. Soon the two of you are glorying in the mysteries of benign cysts and calcium deposits that cloud up an X-ray like the milky-way.

Socorro, succor. Assistance in times of distress, you think, peaceful as your own breasts are being crushed between the metal hands of the mammogram machine.

One day Peter returns from Brazil.

"It's over," you say.

"What do you mean?"

"I've had it up to here. Teaching Shakespeare at a prep school. I've decided to volunteer at Enlace Comunitario. They need some English as a Second Language teachers. It's your turn to get a day job, Peter. It's my turn to live my dream."

"I'll look at the classifieds tonight. Jeez, I thought you were about to ask for a divorce."

"Don't exhale just yet."

"What?"

"Today, no Cory for short. Just for this day I want to hear you call me Socorro. All my life I've—."

Peter draws you into his arms. Cory, that dry shrub of a name, floats away as Peter, with a kiss, draws out the succulence of the name you had almost lost.

After making love, you walk with him around the corner to El Bandido. As always you order water, *agua, por favor,* but this time, without ice, *sin hielo.* Before, you had only enough words to get half way across a situation, like a car stuck on the railroad tracks. You were unable to cry help in any language that might save you.

A steaming platter of shrimp arrives at the table with *tortillas de maiz, frijoles de olla,* and *pico de gallo.* Across from you on the wall hangs an Aztec calendar. "Here's to my other ancestors. We'll study their language, Nahuatl, together," you say, the lip of your wineglass touching Peter's. At last you have discovered the opening in the fence that divides Mexico from the United States, kin from kin, era from era. *Tlen titlatoa moyollo?* What does your heart say? your ancestors ask. The opening was there all along at the tip of your tongue.

◆

My little Destiny,

This is a sad day for your Mama. Your Papa, my beloved Marcos, has had to go back to the land of his birth, El Salvador. He has saved up enough money to build his Mama a real house. She's been living in a house made of sticks and stones, but with his background in construction he will build something most wondrous and worthy. When he comes back he will make haste to find work again and we shall move in together—as it costs much to bring a child into this world of dreadful financial woes. Peter says over and again that capitalism is in its death throes. I for one pray a Hail Mary each night for the end of capitalism as we know it. But I hope it doesn't happen too soon. For your Mama has come up with a plan to turn a little profit, that we might live more comfortably. It came to me a few weeks ago that I could sell Avon on the side to the ladies at La Tropical. Just yesterday three waitresses abandoned their dark red lipsticks for Avon's Wild Orchid, a color much more in the pink family. Their lips, instead of receding into their faces, pop out nice and full and youthful. I have started a trend!

In the meantime, though we feel sorrow today, we must continue waiting patiently and with good cheer for Papa to come home. We must contemplate the good things. We must be grateful always, for despite these hard times we eat well. Blessed are we Mexicans, for our humble beans and corn tortillas form a complete protein, according to the wisdom of the Creator.

Well, little one, I had better stop here. I need to get out and walk around the block to pass out brochures on Auto Theft Prevention, How to Report a Crime and Be a Good Witness, Identity

Theft, and Personal Safety. A Block Captain must keep up on all the literature. But I'd better move quickly as it will be dark soon and I would be embarrassed unto death if a murderer or thief got his hands on me, the Block Captain, who strains to set good examples for one and all. Off I go.

Love,

Your Mama

Dream Time

Maritza

The dream is the same for three nights in a row. Your friends are gathered round a giant clay horno, an oven shaped like a beehive that was used to bake bread outdoors in the old days. It's the same horno your great-grandma used to bake perfect, round loaves behind her farmhouse in Los Lunas, just south of Albuquerque.

Flor, Cory and Lupe are there, staring at the mouth of the horno. Flor starts to pace. Cory bites her nails. Lupe makes the sign of the cross.

Gripping a long-armed paddle, Lupe squats down to get a better look inside. "Come on, come on," she whispers, wiping the sweat off her forehead. "Time!" she shouts as she slips the paddle beneath the bread and carefully draws out the steaming brown loaf.

"It's a girl!" Flor shouts.

"*Una niña!*" Cory translates.

"Made in the USA!" says Lupe, waving a birth certificate.

The dream ends with you in a hospital bed surrounded by your friends, who have just witnessed the birth of your child. But the baby is not in the scene. You call out her name. "Soledad!" Your friends are silent. Maria, your curandera, appears at the bedside dressed in black. She takes your hand and says, "She's with God." She says more, but all you hear is static. You touch your stomach and cry out.

You wake up, tears hot on your face. Flor is asleep, her hair swirled over her breasts like a black rebozo. You stare out the window. The sun is making its slow ascent over the east flank of the blue Sandia Mountains. When the light spills over into dawn, Flor opens her eyes.

"Morning, babe," she says. She picks up her watch from the bed-side table. "It's early. Let's go back to sleep."

"I had that dream again—about the horno. I have to find out what it means."

You are the granddaughter of a woman who prayed in tongues at the Spanish Assembly of God Church, a woman who believed God spoke to ordinary people in dreams. When she came to the United States from Chihuahua as a young woman, she taught herself to read and write. As an adult, after giving her life to God, she recorded her dreams in a twenty-five-cent spiral notebook, which she kept beneath her Bible.

"I can't imagine what the dream means," Flor says. "You've never wanted children. On our very first date you said that when God made you, he forgot to set the alarm on your biological clock. I think you should call Natasha."

Natasha has been Flor's therapist for years. But you don't believe in therapy. You believe in ceremony. You would call Maria now except that she is in Mexico to see family and speak at a meeting of traditional healers and medical doctors. You decide to leave a message on her answering machine.

"Hello, Maria. It's Maritza. I'm calling to set up a time—."

"Hola, hola," Maria says. "Hang on. Let me turn this doggone machine off."

"Maria, I'm sorry for calling this early. I thought you were away."

"Not to worry, little sister. I got home Friday. I was just about to go outside to get my *Albuquerque Journal*. I like to read it with my morning coffee. Obituaries first, of course." She chuckles. "I have to see what my good friend, Doña Sebastiana, is up to."

You picture Doña Sebastiana, famous in New Mexican art: a skeleton dressed in black, riding a cart and holding a bow and arrow. Her name is a nickname for death.

"And you, Maritza, what on earth are you doing up at this ungodly hour?"

"I need to make an appointment with you, Maria. I've had this dream. Three nights in a row. It, well it . . ." You can't continue, tears well up, your sentences are snapping in two. "Maybe it's trying to tell me something."

"Appointment nothing. Get yourself over here now. Dreams are always trying to tell us something."

On the drive to Maria's house, rain clouds choke the sky. Cars whiz by, their lights like stars poking holes in the foggy dark. Too exhausted to stay tethered to the present, you think back to when you were nineteen years old. You remember the pale elderly woman at the pro-life clinic. She was sorting and folding diapers and bibs when you signed in and sat down on a plastic chair. You were the only one in the waiting room. You went to the Life First Clinic because it was within walking distance. The clinic offered free pregnancy tests. Finally, the woman called your name and asked for some details. You said your period was almost two weeks late. "Honey," she said, "it's probably too early to tell. Come back in another week. Everything is going to be alright." She smiled reassuringly and handed you a brochure. "Just remember. Abortion is murder."

You waited for her to say more, to paint a picture of babies bouncing blissfully on hips in a universe where the poor had finally inherited the earth. More than ever you wanted to believe. Your boyfriend had up and moved out. You were late on the rent payment, working a minimum wage job.

The brochure had a smiling, blonde baby on the cover. The infant looked like the baby on a flight you had taken once to Phoenix. Screaming in his mother's arms beside you, you quieted him by playing peekaboo for over an hour. After the plane landed the passengers gave you a standing ovation. Southwest Airlines presented you with a ticket good for any flight taken within the next dozen years.

"I love children," you said, looking at the brochure. "I don't want to murder them," you said to the elderly woman. But when you looked up, you saw that she had turned away and was deep in her diapers and bibs. You headed for the nearest restroom.

You sat down on the toilet. On the wall opposite you, at eye level, was a photo of an embryo blown up a hundred times its normal size. It looked like a monster shrimp. You forgot that you needed to pee. You ran out of the clinic and all the way home.

A week later you took the bus to the Your Choice Clinic. The test came back positive. You looked down at your sweaty palms as if this moment should have been foretold: At age nineteen you will come to a fork in the road called hell. You looked up as the woman scribbled something in your chart. Surely comfort is at hand, you thought. Surely the clinic worker will put her arm around you, tell you sisterhood is powerful, and tell you about the time that she too had to make a painful decision to end a pregnancy or give a newborn up for adoption.

The worker looked at her watch. "We close in five minutes," she said. Handing you brochures, she said, "These will tell you where to get an affordable abortion should you go with that option, or how to enroll in a program that offers discount health care until the baby is born." You felt like you had been handed a menu. You glanced down at your options but couldn't see through your tears.

One week later, alone and scared, feet in stirrups, you stared at a poster taped to the ceiling—a picture of a stand of redwood trees—and listened to what sounded like a dentist's drill as a doctor brought the beginning of a mystery within you to an end.

◆

"Come in, come in," Maria says. She's wearing jeans and an orange Mexican blouse embroidered with hummingbirds. Her braid, which normally snakes down her back, is tied up in a bun. "Let's sit here in the kitchen. It's warm and cozy. After we talk, I'll fry us up some eggs."

You sit down at a small, round table and take a look around. On top of the refrigerator is a statue of the dark-skinned Lady of Guadalupe, who appeared to the Aztec Indian, Juan Diego, and spoke his language, Nahuatl. Beside her is Coatlique, an Aztec goddess wearing a skirt made of serpents. Next to the sink is Maria's black and white TV. Her favorite Spanish-language preacher is on, the sound muted. An interpreter for the deaf stands next to the pulpit, her hands dancing.

Maria pulls a chair up close to you then recites a long prayer, invoking the presence of God, angels, saints, spirits, and ancestors. "Now tell me about the dream, little sister," she concludes. "Speak to me from the heart."

You describe the dream of the horno in detail. Maria hands you a napkin to wipe your tears.

When you're done, Maria stuns you with a simple question: "How old were you when you had an abortion?"

"I was nineteen."

Maria lowers her head and closes her eyes. Then she looks up at Our Lady of Guadalupe, who wears the Aztec sash symbolizing pregnancy. Or maybe she's looking at the serpent-skirted Coatlique, mother of the Aztec god Huitzilopochtli, who sprang full grown from his mother's womb, dressed as a warrior.

Maria takes your hand. "If you're looking to me for forgiveness," she says, "forget about it. Now I want you to listen closely. What we're going to do now is a process of elimination, theologically speaking."

Sensing that you are about to enter a labyrinth you squeeze her hand, determined not to get separated.

"First step, science. Science came along, tool kit in hand," Maria begins. "Before we knew what hit us—the human race—we had pictures. Pictures of the moon. Pictures of the earth from space. Pictures of embryos. All very advanced. And thus it was that science informed us that abortion stops a beating heart. No contradiction there.

"But long before science there were stories. Beliefs, we'll call them, about when God breathed a soul into flesh. Different religions gave us different opinions: The soul swoops down at quickening, at birth, 130 days after birth, and on and on endlessly unto this day. Throughout history our own Catholic Church has changed its almighty opinion as to when this ensoulment business happens. You can look it up in the library. It's declassified, as they say."

Maria bows her head again, whispers something to herself, then looks up. "Now on to God himself. Tell me. Is our Lord so puny and mean-hearted that he would condemn a young woman, scared and confused? A woman, it should be added, who would grow up to perform good works, keeping the Peace Center in the black, year after year?

"Did the ancestors condemn to hell my great-grandma who died on account of a botched abortion because she could not feed the children she already had?"

Maria pauses for a long time, preparing it seems for her closing arguments. "As testified to by science, you stopped a beating heart. But if I had a million dollars, I'd bet every centavo of it that Jesus was looking down at you in that doctor's office. True to his personality, he suffered with you, never abandoning you. Do we know if there was a soul in that fetus? No, we don't. But if there was one, the gods of all our ancestors surely told it to fly away for the time being."

Maria stands up and walks toward the television set. Beside it is an ashtray holding a bundle of cedar or sage, you're not sure which. She lights it on the flame of the gas stove. "*Levántate*, little sister," she says. You stand up and face her. You feel like you are first in line before God on the judgment day, desperate to learn if your name is inscribed in the Book of Life. Slowly, Maria walks around you, blowing the incense toward your body. The smell of it takes you back to your grandmother's kitchen where *atole*—blue corn soup—steamed on the stove while she sat at the table writing in her book of dreams.

You're called back to present time by Maria's gentle command: "Okay, *hermanita*, make the sign of the cross to bless the four directions of your beautiful life."

You do so slowly, returning to the crossroads, all possibilities opening again.

"Good, now a deep breath," Maria says, "and a smile." The two of you embrace. "You've been on a long, long journey. It's time for you to eat."

Maria returns the smoking bundle to the ashtray and stamps it out. She pours oil in a frying pan, cracking open eggs from the hens she keeps in her back yard.

You lean back against the kitchen chair. The preacher on TV is wiping the sweat from his brow with a handkerchief. He turns the pages of his Bible. He points to a passage, looks up, and speaks. You try to read his lips. You wish you understood the sign language interpreter, who is smiling, the world in her hands. She knows the secret alphabet of forgiveness and love. You look forward, clear-eyed, to the rest of your life.

◆

My Dearest Destiny,

Today I will record the improbable tale of how I came to master the English language. I was born on the outskirts of Nogales, Sonora, to Maria Anaya, who is your grandma, her full name being Maria de Jesús. We lived in a Colonia named for the saint of hopeless causes, San Judas Tadeo. Poor and desperate like everyone else in our beloved barrio, your grandma and I schemed to improve our lot. Mama prayed and wept, imploring San Judas and her dead husband, my papa, to intervene before our Lord on our behalf. Then it came to her. She arose one day at five in the morning and from the ice box produced a batch of maize and lard. It remains to this day a mystery how she made dough into tamales too numerous to count. She was a great believer in the multiplication of the loaves, as reported in the Gospels, so I suppose I should not have been bewildered.

After I rolled out of bed at seven in the morning, my mama declared, We shall open an eatery. We shall call it Casa Maria, she said, handing me crayons and a scrap of board to make a sign. By nine in the morning she had arranged in our kitchen plastic chairs and tables she had resurrected over the years from a hotel Dumpster. But how will people know about our enterprise? I asked her. Shouldn't we have publicity? Good idea, said she. Go house to house, give away free sticks of gum and tell all, she commanded. This I did: at fifteen years of age my first job, public relations. Soon our neighbors filled our shack with a joyful noise. They watched the soccer games and *telenovelas* on our black and white. They ate tamales and beans and paid their pesos. Also, we sold soda pop, candies, piñatas, and the like. Mama's reputation as tamale chef spread across the land. Before we knew what hit us, the rich ladies from the parish were ordering tamales from Mama by the dozen.

We were happy. We ate well. We loved our neighbors as ourselves. So you can imagine our sorrow when many of our customers from all around San Judas began to cry farewell, their faces in their hands. Free Trade, Free Trade! they cried. Thanks to the North American Free Trade Agreement, as it is called in full, many of our finest young men were leaving their families and crossing the border in search of work. This free trade business, as you will one day learn in college, was supposed to float all our boats, American and Mexican. Instead, jobs drained away. Poof. I feared that one day this too would be my story—I would have to go north to the United States of America to help Mama make ends meet. So I set about with great ambition to get my English vocabulary going, no easy thing.

First I studied cartoons in English on our television set on Saturday while assisting your grandma in running the store. Then I graduated to late night soap operas, watching men and women of the United States fall in and out of love, mostly out. Then, to my great pride, I began listening to news from the United States White House, at the home of a neighbor who had fancy cable TV. Sure it was a lot of politicians lying, thought I, but they were lying in English. Good enough for me.

But my truly advanced skills came thanks to the Pilgrimage House, around the corner from our store. Young Christian people from all over the United States came to Nogales every month to study injustice. They viewed the Colonia where we lived and took careful notes about poverty. They talked to workers and bosses at the maquiladora factories. Then they visited our little store where they bought tamales and bottled water. Speak to us of your experiences, they pleaded. And so I did, with my still shaky English, with an interpreter when I needed help. I told them of life in Colonia San Judas. How I had to drop out of school to help mama. How mama worked weekends cleaning the houses of rich people. How the maquiladoras were closing down and going to China. The young Christians clapped their hands after I testified. I felt proud to aid in their education. I became a fixture on their monthly tours.

Soon the young people were inviting me to Pilgrimage House on weekends to sing spirituals with them and to study what the Bible says about how the poor will inherit the earth. This we did with much prayer and testimony of conversions to Jesus, a poor carpenter who declared that rich people would have to pass through the eye of a needle to make it to heaven. These prayer meetings were like the tent revivals of old. Tears and laughter. Raised hands and halleluiahs. Love of God and hatred of Free Trade. And hormones swarming like bees.

So it was that every few months a boy fell for me—and hard. Don't get wrong impressions. These were good Christians. There behind the Pilgrimage House we kissed, keeping everything above the waist. Many a boy declared his love for me. Oh Guadalupe, said they, I cannot live without you. But I knew better. I was the Spanish lesson they'd been dreaming of without even knowing it. After the boys returned to the United States they wrote letters to me in English at my request, sometimes for months. I wrote back in Spanish. It was fair trade. Or maybe not. My English got better than their Spanish. Way faster. No secret to it. These young Christians just wanted to change the world. I wanted to change my life.

So there you have it, my little Destiny. Your mama's ambitions to learn English paid off handsomely. I function now in two languages, which you too shall do one day. For this reason I went to the library and managed to check out a bilingual copy of Harry

Potter. It is slow going, this business of reading to you a page in English, and then the translated page in Spanish. And as if all this wasn't enough, Cory and Peter tell me I must play Mozart, too, as I fall asleep, to jump-start your brain even more. We won't tell them that we prefer mariachi music to get that brain of yours going. Okay, here I shall sign off, as I must put on my uniform and head out to La Tropical. I am helping Mr. Simmons develop a recipe for enchiladas with tofu and vegetables instead of cheese, as some of our customers have gone vegan on us. Oh well, we must be ecumenical in our customer service. But tofu enchiladas? What is this world coming to?

Love,

Your Mama

PS: My new campaign as Block Captain is to talk the ladies of the block out of carrying purses, a target for robbers. They can carry their valuables—money, credit card, and wallet—in pockets or, for that matter, in their bras as we did in the days of old. This will be hard work, changing minds and habits, so wish your mama luck, who seeks only to serve mankind in her simple way, saving residents from the darkness of crime, and teaching them to look out for one another, in sickness and in health.

Prayer Wheels

Flor and Lupe

"I've had it up to here, Flor, selling Avon to the other waitresses at La Tropical, poor as me," Lupe says. "Last night I found myself thinking, this is the United States of America. There must be a better way. So I prayed. And believe it or not, Flor, I had a vision."

I look at my beloved friend watering geraniums, blooming in coffee cans in her screened-in front porch, and wonder what on earth God has told her this time around.

Last year she called Maritza and me at six in the morning to invite us to a "garden party." Next thing we know she's handing out shovels to us and Cory and Peter so that we can tear up her dirt yard, which is about the size of a postage stamp.

She'd had a dream of a garden, she told us, a warning from the Lord that we must be more self-reliant, because food would soon be as costly for Americans as it is for Mexicans. Before long she'd grown enough vegetables to meet her needs. The extra squash found its way into pots of soup at the Catholic Worker House. That's Lupe for you. Making miracles happen, but giving God all the credit.

"A vision, huh? Sounds like serious business." I take my cell phone out of my back pocket and turn it off. Lupe sits down beside me and takes a long sip of lemonade. She closes her eyes then strokes her belly, bigger by the day with the baby she has named Destiny. Lupe is quiet for so long that I wonder if she has fallen into a trance.

But then she begins to talk. "There I was, kneeling beside my bed. 'Oh Lord,' I said, 'you alone know my sad secret. This child

---

began her journey to earth because I forgot to take a pill, pure and simple.'"

"'Oh Lord', I prayed on, 'your only begotten son preached that the poor shall inherit the earth. I humbly ask you to distribute some of that earthly wealth my way. Delay not. Babies cost. Big time. Amen.'"

Lupe falls silent, her eyes closed. After a while I wonder if she has fallen asleep. Or maybe her blood sugar has dropped. I consider shaking her—but she resumes her tale.

"And so it was that I stood up to go to the bathroom to get ready for bed. But no sooner had I opened the jar of Ponds cold cream, than I saw it. There in the bathroom mirror, a vision was given to me of dozens of round birth control compacts, each adorned with— adorned with . . ."

Lupe's eyes pop open. She turns to me, her face pale.

"What Lupe, what? Adorned with what?"

Still pale, she makes the sign of the cross.

"Each birth control packet bore a picture of Our Lady."

"Which lady?"

"All of them. Our Lady of Guadalupe. Our Lady of Perpetual Help. Our Lady of Sorrows. Our Lady of Fatima, and Lourdes, and more still, whose blessed names I cannot now recall."

Lupe presses her hand against her chest. I'm afraid she might hyperventilate and pass out.

"I held on to the edge of the sink and sank down on my knees to pray. But no sooner had the words 'Hail Mary' come out of my mouth, than it came to me—the answer to my prayers, the meaning of everything.

"I opened the cabinet under the sink. I reached behind the toilet paper. Then I pulled it out—the plastic bag filled with what I need to save me from a life of everlasting poverty."

Lupe stops talking and leans toward me. The color is back in her face. She takes my hand then looks around, as if someone might be hiding among the geraniums.

"You must promise not to say a word to anyone about this except Maritza. I tell you, if some gringo gets hold of my money-making idea, it will be the end of everything."

"*Te prometo*, Lupe. Lips sealed."

Lupe stands up and yanks a dead leaf off one of her plants. She locks her screen door. She starts pacing the porch.

"You know how I hang on to beautiful junk, thinking something might come in handy for a crafts project. Below the sink I've saved dozens of empty birth control packets."

Lupe's hand disappears into her apron pocket then emerges with a round, pink object, which she holds up like a trophy. She sits down and sets it gingerly in my open palm. This is the first time I've ever held a birth control packet. I contemplate the man-made miracle that allows women to clock their cycles as the moon once did for them.

"Here's the plan for my creation," Lupe says, tapping the packet. "We decorate the covers of these with pictures of Our Lady." Lupe opens the packet. "On the inside cover we inscribe, with magic markers, inspirational sayings from the Bible. You know, like, 'Be not afraid,' or 'Your faith has healed you.'"

Lupe pauses, moved I imagine by the power of the word of God— or by the prospect of making millions as banks go begging for bail-outs.

I run my finger along the circle of clear plastic slits, now empty, where the pills once belonged. "And here?"

"In place of the pills we will have beads of every color set with clear glue. The day-of-the-week sticker encircling the slits stays put. On Monday, a woman reads the inspirational quote then pops the bead out, like it was a pill. On Tuesday, she turns the wheel and meditates yet again on the blessed words. She pops the bead out. On Wednesday the same. And so on for twenty-eight days."

Lupe takes the packet from me and holds it open, close to her face.

"She can do this ritual in the privacy of her home—when she's on the phone, stuck on hold. She can do it in the bathroom stall at work or if she's stuck in a traffic jam. She can open her compact while waiting in line at the grocery store. Everyone will think she's looking in a mirror, checking her lipstick, when in fact she is filling her head with holy wisdom, mantras that have carried us through this vale of tears for millennia and that remain relevant even now, Flor, in these end times."

She snaps the packet shut. "Not bad, huh," she says, smiling, "for a Mexican who could have perished walking across the border to get to these United States? I tell you, in these end times—."

"Hang on, Lupe. Let me get us some more lemonade."

I head slowly toward the refrigerator. The last thing I want is to get Lupe going on the end times. She reads the *Albuquerque Journal* every day, clipping articles about climate change, food shortages, the oil wars in which we are now mired, the water wars yet to come, and the disappearance of bees, forests, and coral reefs. One day I asked her about her strange hobby. "Poor people have always experienced the end times," she said. "Now even the rich can't escape them. Maybe I'm sinning, but it makes me feel good to know that."

I take the pitcher to the porch along with a bag of potato chips and refill our glasses.

"And at the end of twenty-eight days, Lupe, what happens, besides enlightenment?"

"I'll tell you what happens," she says. "Our customer, having drunk deeply of the spiritual life, will go to the Lupe's Prayer Wheels website. She will order another prayer wheel, with a new image and Bible verse, at twenty dollars a pop, plus shipping and handling. For twenty-five dollars, our customer may provide a picture of her favorite guru and a copy of his or her holy words, and we will custom-make a prayer wheel. We must tailor our product for all God's children.

"Not only that. We'll give our customers a discount if they return the used packet and beads so they don't end up in the landfill. After all, saving our poor planet is finally the 'in' thing.

"Shoot, there's that fly again." Lupe grabs a flyswatter from beside her chair and takes aim—then spares the creature in order to open the door for her mailman. "Juan, what's the good word?" she asks. "Not much today that's good," he says. "*La migra* raided the poultry factory in the South Valley."

She steps outside and Juan updates her about this latest scandal. Undocumented workers were rounded up, as was the mayor. He had just arrived to meet the press and boast about the city's superior workforce for a story about local businesses in the *Albuquerque Journal's* business section.

The birth control packet, resting on the table next to Lupe's lime-green pitcher, makes me think of a castanet awaiting the hand of a flamenco dancer to bring its music to life. It's not out of the realm of possibility that Lupe might one day be selling her prayer wheels at the Spanish Market in Santa Fe. Her Destiny might have been a mistake but she might well be the best mistake Lupe has ever made. Because my friend is nothing if not a go-getter. She can turn her luck around, turn *caca* into cash. There's no other way to say it.

Lupe brings her mail in and reminds me that the price of stamps will be going up one penny as of tomorrow. She sits down again and drops the mail beside her on the floor.

"So how much start-up money will you need for your project, Lupe?"

"Fifty dollars."

"And how much do you have in savings?"

"Fifty dollars," she says, lowering her voice to a near whisper.

"The money is in a tampon box in the drawer where I keep my bathroom towels. Remember that in case something happens to me."

"Fifty doesn't seem like much money."

"No, but it will go a long way. For one thing we don't have to *buy* pictures of Our Lady. What we do is hit up the funeral homes. You might not know this, Florita, because you're Jewish. But at Catholic funerals they hand out free holy cards. Each one has a picture of Our Lady—and the name of the dearly deceased on the other side. I'll bet they have loads of extras to spare for a good cause.

"As for beads we go to Beads Unlimited. And I've already got oodles of beads from broken earrings that I've saved year in and year out for a moment such as this. For glue and varnish we go to Hobby Lobby. And I want to pay Maritza to set me up a website."

"Don't be silly, Lupita. She'll do it for free. And let me invest the fifty."

It's hard to believe that I've just volunteered to part with fifty dollars for an untested venture. I'm the kind who knows exactly what I'd do if I were to win the lottery: pay off my house as well as the Peace Center's mortgage and buy health insurance for all my activist friends. The problem is, I've never purchased a lottery ticket in my life. "Why waste the money?" I always tell Maritza. "I'd rather buy a *New York Times*."

But Lupe's plan appears to be so well thought out, I half-expect her to hand me a typed-up projection of annual earnings.

Lupe stretches her legs out and rubs her tummy as if it were a crystal ball.

"I tell you Flor, I smell money, and that doesn't happen very often. My prayer is that I will one day hire others to help me put these things together—a cottage industry for the wretched of the earth, like me."

Lupe slips the birth control compact back into her apron pocket.

"Besides, it's about time our poor *raza* cashes in. Look at the gringos—including many of our dearest friends—wearing beads on their wrists that they use to say their Buddhist prayers. God only knows what those things sell for. And us Chicanos and Mexicanos? The years pass and our rosaries sway uselessly from our cars' rearview mirrors. All this time we could have prepared the way of the Lord—hightailing it to the Santa Fe flea market.

"From the backs of our trucks we could have sold *los rico*s of Santa Fe thousands of rosaries, twenty dollars a pop, that they could wrap around their wrists. And in their darkest hours they would remember to say their Hail Marys and Our Fathers. Or chant their Oms, bead by bead."

Lupe's up again, pacing on her swollen feet with her flyswatter.

"And you know why no one else has come up with this idea, Flor? It's because our people think too much about Almighty God and not enough about the almighty dollar."

She sits down, reaches into her pocket and pulls out a rosary. She holds it up and watches it sway back and forth. Its hypnotic motion appears to release my friend from her agitated state.

"Hand me the potato chips," she says, dropping the rosary on her lap.

We munch in silence. The Spanish broom in Lupe's yard, gloriously yellow, perfumes the porch with each breeze.

"Lupe, you've had a full day. You go put your feet up."

Lupe yawns. She cracks her knuckles. "I should, Florita. Tell Maritza our good news. Thanks be to our Lord that the idea for Lupe's Prayer Wheels came from Him, for my mind is too weak."

Warn Maritza is more like it, I think, as I give Lupe an *abrazo* and head out. I can see it now, the three of us bent over Lupe's kitchen table, gluing Mary's face on little plastic packets—for all we know making art history worthy of Judy Chicago—or more likely calling down the wrath of some obscure right-wing element of Lupe's parish, Our Lady of the Lake.

"The bishop," says Maritza, standing beside the bed. It's Sunday, six in the morning.

"What?"

"As in the Archbishop of Santa Fe." She holds up the front page of the *Albuquerque Journal* at arm's length, as if it were a blanket infested with smallpox.

"Give it here."

The headline is so large that I don't need my reading glasses. "Archbishop O'Connor Says Art Project 'Scandalous,' Urges Boycott."

Maritza takes the paper from me and reads the accompanying article out loud. The paper quotes Lupe—a statement that Maritza wrote up and had her memorize in case someone at the Spanish Market might be offended by the project:

"'An empty birth control compact is a morally neutral object. Faced with the decision to transform it into a spiritual aid—or to add it to the landfill—I chose the former. Our Holy Father recently defined destruction of the environment as a sin. I had no choice in the matter.'"

A photograph of Lupe's smiling face appears with that of her partner in sin, the acclaimed artist, Goldie Garcia.

We had drawn in our friend Goldie after a week of Mary's faces peeling off plastic, beads popping out of their sockets, and biblical consolations liquefying under our brushes as we coated them with varnish. Not long after Goldie got involved, the prayer wheels were being picked up by a Santa Fe gallery in limited editions. They were juried into the Spanish Market.

"What are we going to do?" Maritza says, shaking the newspaper. "This is just awful. Lupe will be devastated."

"Well, I guess we should call her before she goes out and gets the paper."

We look at the phone on the bedside table. Neither of us makes a move. Then we both reach for the phone—but before we can pick it up it rings. Maritza pulls her hand away. I pick up the receiver and press the speakerphone button.

"Did you see the paper? *Es un milagro.* I tell you there is a God, after all. *Santa Maria!*" Lupe shouts, swimming between two languages as she does whenever she is elated. "We've struck gold! I must have a hundred emails, with requests for prayer wheels and interviews. They're going to do a story about me and Goldie on Univisión. *Gracias a Dios en los cielos.* My Destiny will be okay."

She hangs up so she can call Goldie.

"She did it," I tell Maritza after she climbs back in bed, tossing the paper on the floor. "Yes," Maritza answers. She turns over on her side, pulls up close and kisses me on my forehead. A long silence follows. "I had a dream last night, Flor. I know you don't believe in these sorts of things, in signs, but, well . . ." "Go ahead love," I tell her. "Well, the dream was more like a snapshot. I saw barbed wire. And I understood that the wire had somehow been transformed into guitar strings."

Neither of us says a word for a long time. To my surprise tears sting my eyes. Maritza continues. "We may never really know what Lupe went through. Crossing the border on foot. Walking through the desert. Whenever I ask all she says is, 'Oh it was no biggie, Mari. I was dumb enough to drink from a barrel where the cows drink. Some nice people found me and gave me fresh water and that was the end of it.'"

I wipe my eyes with the back of my hand. "Why don't we hold a surprise party for Lupe and Goldie on a Friday evening. We'll say we're having them over for Sabbath supper. When we're done blessing the tortilla and wine, our friends will come out of the bedroom and yell, Surprise!"

Maritza sits up. Her amber eyes shine as she watches sunlight streaming through bamboo blinds. "So you think my dream was a sign? God didn't exactly part the Rio Grande for Lupe so that she could cross. But something happened. The barbed wire . . ."

Maritza's voice trails off.

"I don't know what to think, Mari. But I believe, whatever that means. Hand me that notebook on the bedside table. Let's make a guest list for the party."

◈

My Dearest Destiny,

Your mama is not doing so well today. Morning sickness has turned into all day sickness, about which the experts offer little consolation or advice. Three times I served our long-suffering customers huevos rancheros topped with red chile made with pork, when in fact they had asked for the vegetarian-style option. The rules say we must throw away bad orders, even if untouched. But Mr. Simmons took pity on me. "Guadaloopy," he said, "take that good food home. You need it, you're pregnant." Then he relieved me of having to tend to customers. Instead, today I get to wipe down tables, booths, and counters, chop lettuce, and sweep out the back room. And so it is that I sit here on a box packed with cans of jalapeños to write you this note, despairing though it is. Your mama had high hopes that she could make enough money off her art work, Lupe's Prayer Wheels, so that she could quit this job. But this infernal recession has kept sales down. Not only that but two of your aunts, Concepcion and Rosario, lost their jobs at the maquiladora. So it falls to me to send as much money home as possible, to help out Mama and now my two sisters, as well. I must close shortly, as Mr. Simmons will surely show up to ask after my health. If he sees me without the broom, no more job for me. You have never seen so much dirt. I cannot stop coughing, and I worry that the dust will sneak its way into your lungs too, along with my despair. No, I must stand up straight, go forth, and take heart. Tonight your mama, the Block Captain, has invited the people of the block to a speech about mail piling up. It appears that many of my neighbors do not daily clean out their mailboxes, except for the important items, leaving the junk mail stuffed in the box. This gives awful impressions to thieves, who day and night roam about spying upon houses to break and enter. Mail piled up? The owner is gone on vacation, thinks the thief, as he circles the house for an opening so that he can take what he will, giddy with glee. I will make notes on index cards so as to sound more articulate than I really am. It is the duty of the Block Captain to put the fear of the Lord in the minds of neighbors, so as to keep them safe. I am proud that I can help mankind in this small way, for God has been good to me and I must give something back. Okay now, back to the broom. The studies say exercise is good for pregnant ladies. I will try to recall this when I go under the shelves and sweep up the dead roaches. Uh-oh, I think I hear Mr. Simmons at the door.

Love,

Your Mama

Translations

——

Peter

A baby is growing wild as a weed inside Cory. She conceived after you wooed her away from her night reading—the Spanish translation of *The Great War for Civilization: Conquest of the Middle East*, Robert Fisk's 1,433-page epic history—not counting bibliography and footnotes. As Cory drifted off to sleep she whispered, Rashid Dahr Mohammed. You tried not to take it personally. You knew if you flipped through the *The Great War* you'd find Rashid in there somewhere. Besides, Cory talked in her sleep all the time. Still, you couldn't resist saying to her, "It's Peter here, honey. Peter." To which she responded, "two-state solution."

A pregnancy test from the pharmacy confirmed the good news. Cory had wanted desperately to get pregnant but had concluded after years of failed attempts that she was too old.

To celebrate, the two of you walk to your favorite restaurant, Mannie's Diner, for breakfast. The very idea of pregnancy has you feeling that you are possessed with mysterious powers; you feel like you are the first man in history to father a child. But you realize there is nothing unique about your accomplishment. At Mannie's, infants are everywhere, their parents tending them like crops upon which their lives depend.

"I've never seen so many babies here before," you tell Cory. "Or maybe I just hadn't noticed."

"Yeah, and they all look alike," she replies. It's true, you think. The infants all resemble dolls with Play-Doh faces and buttons for noses. Only the parents can tell them apart. Their love is a

——

magnifying glass that allows them to distinguish their child from all others, each one unique as a snowflake.

You and Cory take a seat in your favorite booth. As usual, her hair looks slightly windblown. She wears a black sweater with a fake diamond necklace that she bought at a garage sale.

"It will be soon enough for us," she says.

"What do you mean?"

"A kid in a high chair here at Mannie's."

"Yup." You contemplate the wondrous alphabet of DNA, the letters X and Y: two people falling in love then sharing a life sentence in the body of their child.

"I can't wait to see the sonogram," Cory says, after ordering huevos rancheros, eggs over easy. "You know, where the heart goes thump, thump. Like a Mexican jumping bean."

You order a stack of pancakes. "All I want to see," you answer, "is the blue birth spot at the base of the spine." You think of the mysterious spot that so many Asian, Indian, and Chicano babies are born with, proof of some ancestral connection, a spot that with time fades away.

"So what does your intuition say?" you ask. "Is it a girl or a boy?"

"I should consult the tarot first," Cory says, "before I give a definitive answer." She fishes around in her huge purse for her deck. "Damn, I left it at home when I picked up the car keys."

You reach into your pocket and pull out a nickel. "This will do for now. Heads, it's a girl. Tails, it's a boy."

You flip the coin. Heads it is.

"Do you have any ideas for names?"

Cory closes her eyes. She takes a deep breath. You imagine her fishing around her subconscious which is as full of odds and ends as her purse. You wonder how she can find anything.

She opens her eyes. She grins. "Lucy," she says.

"Lucy?"

"Lucy. It just came to me, an unexpected inspiration. Think about it. It's easy to pronounce. You can Hispanicize it into Lucía, accent mark over the *i*. Her Spanish nickname would be Luz, light. And Lucy was the name of my grandmother."

Cory taps her fingers on her coffee cup. "Besides," she adds somberly, "Lucy was a saint."

Quite a saint, you think. You picture the holy card Cory has of St. Lucy tucked into the frame of her grandma's photograph. The saintly face is turned upward toward heaven; in her hands is a plate upon which rest two eyeballs. The story goes that the Roman emperor Diocletian had St. Lucy's eyes gouged out because she refused to renounce Christianity.

"Grandma used to pray to her for good eyesight. She read the *Albuquerque Journal*, stock exchange columns included, until a week before she died. She never needed reading glasses."

"*Que descanse en paz*," you say, respectful of the dead. Cory pulls her eyeglasses off and with a napkin dabs her tears.

You pat Cory's hand. You don't dare tell her that when you hear the name Lucy, you think of the Beatles song, "Lucy in the Sky with Diamonds," which you and your high school classmates assumed was a reference to LSD.

The waitress returns with huevos rancheros and pancakes. She too is pregnant, her abdomen stretching the seams of her shirt. You feel like pinching her cheek.

"Lucy is a very meaningful name, filled with history," you say solemnly. "I have an idea too. Something I think you'll really like. But I've got to go to the bathroom first. Back in a second."

You walk past tables of Nuevo Mexicanos—Chicanos, Mexicans, Indians—all of whom in one way or another resemble Cory. Skin copper like pennies, hair and eyes the color of nightfall. The languages they speak—English, Spanish, Spanglish, indigenous tongues—blend into a mantra as ancient as the earth. You walk into the bathroom and lock the door, silencing the ancestral chant. You take a piss and wrack your brains, trying to come up with a name. The stakes are high: You're up against a saint, a saucer, and two eyeballs. You wash your hands then exit. A mother and her little girl are waiting in line outside as you leave. "*Ven aca, Xochitl,*" the mother says, taking the girl by her hand. "It's our turn."

You make your way back to the booth. "I've thought long and hard about this," you tell Cory. "Xochitl. That's the name I vote for."

The busboy drops plates on the floor not far from your table. He picks them up, none are broken. The breakfast crowd applauds. Cory leans toward you, oblivious to the commotion. "Could you repeat what you just said?"

"Xochitl." You grab a napkin and write the name out: XOCHITL, then an approximate pronunciation, SO-CHEE-TEAL. You add a smiley face then pass the napkin to Cory.

"It's the Aztec-Mexica word for flower. It often appears with the word 'song.' Flower and song, which in Aztec philosophy evokes poetry, beauty . . ."

Cory studies the napkin. You imagine the napkin is made of *amatl*, mulberry bark, used by the Aztecs to write their histories before the Spaniards burned their libraries to the ground.

Cory looks up at you and blinks. "You've got to be kidding." She folds the napkin and hands it back to you.

"How could I kid about a thing like this? Everything is about roots. I want this child to know where she came from."

The baby in the booth behind you shrieks like a crow.

Cory leans back and lets out a groan.

"Peter, love of my life. Why go all the way back to Mesoamerica, to the Aztecs for heaven's sake? You want a good Indian name? We only have to go thirteen miles south of Albuquerque to Isleta Pueblo. Have you forgotten that my third cousin lives there? We'll name the baby after her. Tiffany."

Cory chuckles. "Yes, a good Indian name. Besides, my *prima* is famous."

You've heard all about Tiffany. She made the news after having fought off a thief with a broomstick at the Albuquerque gas station that she manages. After she had him under the heel of her cowboy boot, she told him off in Spanish, English and her native tongue, Tiwa—a scene filmed by her brother with his cell phone and released to television stations throughout the southwest. Tiffany was hailed as a hero in an editorial in the *Albuquerque Journal*.

"Hell," Cory says, her eyes tearing up with laughter, "we have a real Indian warrior in the family we can name our child after. Besides, I want Tiffany to be one of the godparents, or whatever it is you Quakers have, at her blessing ceremony."

"Shoot, for that matter," Cory continues, "we can tell our Anglo friends that the baby is the great-great-granddaughter of a Cherokee princess. We'll call her Flying Star."

Flying Star is your favorite coffee shop in the Nob Hill district. You try to join in Cory's laughter but you can't. Her laughter is a pool in which the name Xochitl sinks like a stone.

"Ah honey, I'm not making fun of you. Just a little reality check is all."

You poke at your pancakes then put your fork down. "I'm just trying to come up with something original. God bless Grandma, but surely we can do better than Lucy, the patron saint of eyesight. Besides, you're a Buddhist now. Why on earth would sainthood factor into your thinking?"

"You know me," Cory says. "I never met a religion I didn't like."

You think back to Cory's altar on her dresser. When you were dating she had statues there of Jesus, Our Lady of Guadalupe, and St. Anthony, finder of lost things. Then Jesus got demoted, transferred to a bookshelf in the living room with St. Anthony. Our Lady of Guadalupe, meanwhile, was joined by a Star of David—this in honor of ancestors who practiced Judaism in secret back when New Mexico was New Spain, during the time of the Inquisition. Soon Our Lady and the Star were joined by Quan Yin, Mother Meera, and Krishna playing his flute. "Never hurts to hedge your bets," was Cory's reply, when you asked her about the proliferation of gods and gurus.

Recently, Cory distributed her holy objects throughout the house. In their place she put a Gohonzon, the sacred scroll before which she chants. Every morning and again at night Cory sings in a deep robust voice, *Nam Myoho Renge Kyo*. Since she started the practice six months ago, she has seemed more content, centered. Buddhism, you've concluded, fits her. You sense that she'll hang on to it like a good wool sweater that will keep her warm in life's harsh seasons.

"We have plenty of time to decide on names, honey," she says, reaching for your hand. "Heck, for all we know, it's a boy. Remember you told me that I talked in my sleep after we made love? The night we conceived? If it's a boy let's just name the kid Rashid and call it good."

Some ten weeks after your celebratory breakfast at Mannie's, you throw on a sweater and head out in the rain. Bare branches claw at the clouds, which have swallowed up the stars. You head down Central across from the university. You hear a clink of coins. A Native American man is begging, holding out a coffee can. You give him a dollar bill that falls silently into his hand. The clink of change reminds you of your years in Santa Fe. You think of the wealthy people you knew who spent hundreds of dollars for sessions with someone claiming to be a Native American "shaman." Those same people couldn't cough up more than a quarter for a real Indian who needed a meal.

You could have gone that route; you attended workshops on shamanism, only to conclude it was quackery at best and at worst, a rip off of Native American culture. Instead you sought enlightenment in ordinary life. You dreamed of love, marriage, and creating a family.

Today your dream has come to this: Miscarriage, a pool of blood in the toilet, your wife sobbing, blaming herself for not chanting with enough fervor for a successful pregnancy.

You took her in your arms and whispered, "I love you, Cory." You've always believed that those three words, I love you, can put a man on the road to enlightenment—or if used too lightly, can corrode the spirit of a marriage, turning it into a charade. "I love you too, Peter," Cory answered, her arms gripping her stomach as if still holding onto the hope that this was all a mistake, the blood and clotting and cramps meant nothing, a baby was still on the way.

A young couple—they look to be in their twenties—pass you, pushing a stroller. You're in your fifties, fifteen years older than Cory. You wonder if maybe you are defective. Maybe over the years a gene mutated, preventing your seed from being firmly planted in the soil of Cory's being.

You head into the Frontier Restaurant and get in line to order food to take back home for the two of you. Cory is probably chanting about now. It would do me good, you think, to go to the Quaker meeting on Sunday morning and drink in the silence. Or maybe not. Our Quaker God is too quiet, you think. At times like this you want a god who speaks, a god who can be put on trial and forced to justify his existence in the face of tragedy.

You pick up your food and head for the door. To your surprise you see Flor, Maritza and Lupe squeezed together in a booth. "*Sientate*," Lupe says, getting up to give you an *abrazo*. "We just got done with a prayer vigil at the army recruiting station," Lupe says.

"There was a great turnout," Maritza adds. You sit down next to Lupe. You need to tell the women about the miscarriage but now isn't the time, you need more time to grieve in private. "Say Peter," Flor asks, "we have a delegation of mothers coming from Juarez— the ones whose daughters have been murdered. They'll be here in three weeks, speaking at St. Francis church. Do you think you could be their interpreter?"

"Of course. I'd be happy to." You've interpreted at other forums for the mothers of Juarez. You've stood beside them at podiums that look like witness stands, their daughters' photographs hanging on the wall behind them like wanted posters. The women are beyond dreaming of their daughters rising from the dead. All they want is to say their names, to warn the world that there will be more deaths if people do not speak out.

"You're so lucky, Peter," Maritza says, "that you have such a command of Spanish you can do simultaneous translations." You nod but say nothing. The language that burns like a log, warming and lighting up your life, is nothing but a cold ember today. English too. There are no words to comfort Cory or yourself or the women of Juarez. "I'd better get home," you tell your friends. They say good-bye, all smiles, as you turn and walk away, silence the only language that makes sense.

❖

Dearest Destiny,

If only you were here today—what you would behold! Your mama made the morning newspaper again thanks to the Galeria Goldie Garcia open house to be held on Sunday. They reviewed Lupe's Prayer Wheels in the Arts section with high praise all around. Most shocking of all? They've given to calling me an "artist."

I almost collapsed off my chair at the kitchen table in the dawn hours but feared injuring you. So I steadied myself with a cup of manzanilla tea as I resumed my place at the table. I read the review again and with a pencil circled the word "artist." I said it out loud, "artist," to see if it would fit. But in truth it felt like a too-tight pair of shoes. So I said it again, then again, "artist." Say it enough times, I thought, and it will stretch to fit me, big as I am, carrying you around on swollen feet day and night.

All this excitement got me to thinking of the years I worked at the maquiladora in Nogales. There we dedicated our lives to assembling garage door openers, of the remote control kind, much-used here in these United States.

The gringo boss from Dallas, Texas, one day made a surprise visitation. He told us women to stand straight and proud. "You are craftsmen," said he, in bad Spanish. "Technologically speaking you are in a revolution of the cutting edge of remote garage door openers." He went down the line and shook our hands. When he came to me he said, "And you. You have the most radical job of all. Accomplishing the final test. Aiming that remote and pushing that button to make sure it serves humanity right, opening the experimental door. Now tell me your name."

"Guadalupe Anaya," I said.

"Guadaloopy. Congratulations and much positive luck."

"Thank you and have a safe trip back to your Dallas office," I said, in perfect English.

I thought this was the end of his sermonizing. Not so, not a man on a mission who likes big talk and thinks he's memorized another language. "Ladies," said he. "Remember you are ambassadors for this great free trade. In cooperation, all our rafts will rise, United States and Mexico. Onward!" Away he went not even leaving us a friendly gesture, like a box of chocolates or a fruit basket.

So, my Destiny, all this is to say that your mama has graduated from craftsman to artist, a miracle worth our contemplation for years to come. To think your mama had dreams of being a writer so long ago, but it was not to be. Maybe you will pick up on that dream where I left off. Instead of pushing a broom here at La Tropical, you might be sitting in a booth pushing a pen. Okay, my lunch half-hour is almost up. I must report quickly: Your mama, whom God has chosen to serve as Block Captain, may have saved a life. I noticed that old Mrs. Sanchez had not picked up her newspaper yesterday, a task she does promptly every day at six in the morning. By two in the afternoon, her paper was still there, resting in the grass, unread. It came to me that perhaps something dreadful had happened. Maybe Mrs. Sanchez took a fall and could not get up and out of her house. So off I went, crossing the street to her house to knock on doors and peer into windows. Sure enough, there she was on the floor, conscious, thanks be to God, but unable to stand. So I called her daughter (I keep the numbers of next of kin of all the neighbors) who raced to the rescue, unlocking the door and getting Mrs. Sanchez back on her feet. She was fine, complaining only that she had missed her ritual of black coffee and the morning news.

Well, little one, back to work where no one knows I'm an artist *and* a Block Captain. I'm just another Mexican.

Love,

Mama

Fidelities

Maritza and Flor

Maritza and Flor, in a mood to celebrate, meet for dinner at El Patio, the site of their first date.

Mulberry trees strung with soft white lights make everyone look younger. The liver spot on Flor's right cheek vanishes, as does Maritza's streak of gray hair. They find a table outdoors and take a seat, give each other a kiss in the dim halo of light. The waitress comes by, hands out menus, and asks the women if they would care for some water. Due to years of drought, the state passed legislation making it illegal for restaurants to give customers water unless they ask for it. The two women look to the heavens for signs of rain. Nothing.

"We'll have wine," Flor says. "Red."

"We're out of red," says the waitress. "Will white do?"

"Why not?" Flor says.

"Back in a moment."

Maritza turns to Flor. "So what exactly are we celebrating?"

"Who knows?" Flor answers. "The end of capitalism, I guess."

Maritza and Flor are all for the end of capitalism, but they think such a project calls for some sort of plan. The $700 billion bailout of Wall Street has thus far come to nothing. People are losing jobs, houses, pensions. Mexico's leaders are drawing up plans for a border wall of its own, to keep U.S. citizens from sneaking in, in search of work and affordable health care.

The women read over the menu although they already know it by heart.

"What are you going to have?" asks Flor, noting that the price of a chile burger shot up a dollar since last week.

"I can't decide," Maritza says.

The women have been together for years and—except for the enchiladas they had here on their first date—they have never eaten anything at El Patio but huevos rancheros.

The waitress returns with their drinks and pulls out a pad from her apron to take their order.

"You go first, Flor," Maritza says.

Flor looks up at the waitress. "Huevos rancheros, eggs over easy, green chile. Lots of green." She snaps the menu shut.

Maritza and the waitress look at Flor over their reading glasses.

"Are you sure?" they ask Flor in unison. Flor has never ordered huevos rancheros with green chile—only red. She nods in the affirmative. "Well," the waitress says darkly. "It's your decision."

Flor, ever the activist—energized by looming catastrophes—believes this is not the time for the same old thing. People have to get used to change. What with global warming and the economy, food might one day be rationed, she thinks, with no red chile to be had.

The waitress turns to Maritza.

"Let's see," Maritza says. In keeping with tradition she pauses, imagining how good the other entrees must taste, especially the chiles rellenos. She has vowed to try them for years.

"Huevos rancheros, eggs over easy, *red* chile," Maritza says. "Lots of red," she adds, looking over at Flor.

Ever the cautious balancer-of-books, Maritza believes this is no time to order something different given that Iceland, to cite but one example, has just gone bankrupt. How it all adds up she can't say for sure, but she knows to go with her gut.

"You won't be disappointed," sighs the waitress, relieved that in these rocky times, somebody is clinging to convention.

———

"So what should we toast to?" Flor asks, running her finger around the rim of her wineglass.

"I don't know, to survival I guess," Maritza responds, looking down into the clear pool of wine.

Throughout their lives, when the women have heard the word *survival*, they have thought of different things. Flor remembers her grandmother, who survived Hitler's concentration camps. When Maritza hears the word, she thinks of her indigenous ancestors—the many millions who perished throughout the Americas after having had the bad luck to be discovered by Columbus—and the miracle that so many have survived.

But tonight *survival* means something different, something they would never dare to say out loud.

Five years, four months and seventeen days after Bush declared Mission Accomplished—the day of the women's first date—Flor and Maritza have remained faithful to one another. In a world of shattered relationships, theirs has survived, despite their fears, real and imagined.

For a long time, Maritza dreaded going to the New Mexico Educators Federal Credit Union, where her ex-boyfriend, John, once had an account. Before getting out of her car she would take out a red pencil from the glove compartment and dab lips and cheeks, carefully sizing up the results in the rear view mirror. She would enter the bank, dismayed that she was a size larger since she last saw her ex, and look around nervously. But he was never there.

As for Flor, until last spring, she had kept her cell phone on even at night, should the imagined call from her ex-lover ever come. "Hey Flor, it's Maura. My husband's dead. His plane flew into a mountain. I want to see you." Flor dreaded what such a call might stir up in her. Never mind that Maura had moved to Japan to teach English as a second language. The women had been together for a long time.

How can two people deeply in love be prey to old ghosts?

———

"Natasha," Flor said to her therapist, "I'm still coveting a man's wife. Why? Why?"

"Coveting implies lust," said Natasha, pausing a moment to let the words sink in. "But the truth is coveting stems from greed. Wanting what you can't have and don't need." Flor leaned forward in her chair and closed her eyes. She had five minutes left in her session to compute: Coveting minus lust plus adultery equals greed. She looked up at Natasha. "You mean to say all this time I've wanted Maura because she belongs to someone else?" Flor asked, crying into her Kleenex. "I'm no different from a kid who shoplifts at the corner 7-Eleven for the fun of it. Why didn't you tell me so ages ago?"

"I did," Natasha said. "Twelve sessions ago I said as much, according to your chart. You weren't ready to hear me. It's no easy thing, Flor, this business of being human."

Flor stuffed her Kleenex in her pocket and sighed as she wrote out a check.

Like Flor, Maritza also sought out talk medicine—but from a curandera, Maria, who lives in the South Valley.

Maritza stood with her in front of a huge altar lit up by candles and adorned with images of Our Lady of Guadalupe and Aztec deities. Maria burned copal in a small molcajete and circled Maritza, who breathed in the sweet incense. But Maritza was crying so hard that Maria broke with tradition and cut short the opening prayers by ten minutes, down to fifteen seconds. "Oh Guadalupe, Tonantzin, angels and saints, the Holy Child, and Maritza's ancestors, too numerous to name in this painful moment, *help*."

The two women sat down on lawn chairs near the altar. "So tell me little sister," Maria said, "what brings you here today?"

Maritza calmed down as she breathed in the perfume of the copal. "I know it's irrational," she said, "but I'm still obsessed with John. I'm afraid I'll run into him after all these years and he'll think I'm fat."

Maria jotted down some notes then bowed her head, weighing what she had just heard. She looked up. "Little sister, your problem has nothing to do with John. Like so many women who walk into this room, your issue is body image. That's what we have to work on. I want you this week to look around at your beautiful Mexican and Chicana and Indian sisters. We tend to be on the short side, with little in the way of hips—and love handles on our stomachs and backs."

Maria opened Maritza's chart. She pulled out an article from the *Albuquerque Journal* Metro Section, page one, years old. "Besides," she said, holding up the article. "You seem to forget. John's dead."

Maritza had the same article tucked away somewhere in a book at home. "Leading Advocate for the Homeless Dies in Ski Accident," the headline read.

Maria continued. "I could give you a letting-go-of-an-old-lover ceremony. But it's the wrong remedio. Until you love yourself—and the body the heavenly hosts gave you—you will not be at peace. Pray on that this week." The two women got up and hugged. She gave Maritza some copal to take home. Maritza slipped a donation beneath a candle on the altar.

At El Patio the women hold up their glasses and make a toast. "To survival," they say, clicking their glasses. But what do they really want to say? Love is as fragile as a leaf changing colors and about to fall. It is also as mighty as a tree that stands fast through the seasons.

◆

My Dearest Destiny,

I suppose I should get around to telling you about how I met your papa, for it took two, as you will one day learn, to make you, but don't ask me how, as I don't know about science, I only know about love. One fine day a man took a seat by the south window of La Tropical and ordered a cup of coffee, black. "And for lunch?" I asked. "Nothing," said he. He performed this ritual four days in a row. On the fifth day, I served him unasked his coffee, black. "And for lunch?" I inquired. "Nothing," he answered. "Okay, you got it, Mister, Mister—," I said. "Marcos," he said. "Marcos Martinez of San Salvador, El Salvador, at your service." He held out his hand. "I'm Lupe," said I, softly shaking his hand as if afraid it might break, or worse that the moment might shatter. "Lupe Gabriela Anaya of Albuquerque, via Nogales." I looked up, fearful that Mr. Simmons would catch this breach of restaurant etiquette. "I'll take the check," said Marcos. "Write down your phone number on a napkin, if you please. It would be an honor to take you out for lunch." Little Destiny, your fate was sealed, thanks to a $1.27 cup of bad coffee and a mama who had the good sense to inscribe her phone number in her best script. The rest is for future letters, for this story has yet to end. Stay tuned.

Love,

Mama

A Way with Light

Marcos

I love things that stand for forever. Like rings. Rings go round and round and on and on, like eternity. What do you think of this ring? It's made of silver, with turquoise nuggets. I worked extra hours at a construction site to save up money, then bought the ring at Target. Do you think Lupe will like it? When I get down on my knees and ask her to marry me, will she slip the ring on and say yes to eternity?

It's the least I can offer: to accompany her through this brief life that flares up, flickers, then dies. I dream of summer nights on her front porch, the two of us staring out at stars that punctuate the sky. I dream of sipping lemonade and talking about politics or gossiping about our friends. But most of all, I imagine holding Destiny in my hands.

Forever. Yes, I'm ready for it. To be a husband and a father. A provider. I work hard—I'm a construction worker. I love walking around on a rooftop under a blistering sun, my hands scraped and bruised, my face sunburned. Long ago, at the University of El Salvador, I studied to become an architect. My dream was to build schools and hospitals in the poor areas with materials that could withstand earthquakes—beautiful buildings with courtyards filled with light. But my studies came to an end when I, like so many others, had to flee the Salvadoran death squads. But my dream of light was never completely extinguished.

You see, I'm an expert at installing skylights. I get asked to do it all the time. The word is out in the neighborhoods near the University

---

of New Mexico: hire Marcos Martinez! He has a way with light! And oh, how I enjoy telling the professors who hire me what materials I will need. I enjoy watching their eyes glaze over as I explain that besides the skylight, I will need lumber, drywall, roofing paper, roofing nails, 16d galvanized nails, and so on and so forth. I explain that I have some of my own tools for the job: circular saw, hammer, flat pry bar, tin snips, and a utility knife. The professors nod as if they understand me. But they don't. I am more fluent than they. You see, I am trilingual: I speak Spanish, English, and skylights.

After a trip to the hardware store I have at it, cutting through ceiling and roof. By day's end I'm covered with grit but feeling like God, who said let there be light. You probably can't imagine a construction worker feeling like God. Not that brown man on a rooftop you see as you drive on your way to work or to the gym. That brown man—who looks like an illegal alien. Yesterday some high school kids walked by the house I was working on and called me a wetback. "Hey, alien, let's see your documents," they shouted before laughing and moving on.

I wanted to say to them, No human being is illegal. But I stood there mute, salty tears sliding down my face. I've got documents, I wanted to tell them, more than I care to remember. I was a photographer for the university newspaper. I took dozens of pictures of students who had spoken out against the Salvadoran dictatorship. The clearest pictures were the ones I took at the morgue. The florescent light glancing off concrete slabs allowed for the most accurate rendering of a face. I wanted those high school boys to see my work, to meet a man obsessed with documentation: keeping alive forever the memory of El Salvador's dead—thanks to tricks of light and a lens aimed just so.

I'm sorry, I didn't mean to take such a dark turn. It happens to me—life's light goes dim—most often when I'm starting to fall asleep. In fact, I have little to fear. I'm one of the lucky few who got political asylum here in the United States; eventually, I got citizenship. Still, it's hard to shake the old shadows. I have a recurring dream that I'm entering a crawl space to insulate a house. I'm wiping cobwebs off my face, claustrophobic, pointing a flashlight—when up ahead I see a black widow spider dangling from a clod of dirt. In the glare its bulbous body gleams like onyx. I wake up, terrified of falling back to sleep. It all comes back, the distant past: Before I fled El Salvador I was taken prisoner. I was forced to smash my camera with a machete. Then I was put in a cell the size of a coffin; I couldn't even sit up to pee. I escaped after a month. Can you see why I love walking on rooftops, the sun beating down on my face? The world is my cell, measureless and luminous. And I can see everything and everyone. I watch you as you walk outside to get the morning paper, put out the trash, water your plants, drive out of your driveway. Remember my story. Remember to respect the brown man on the rooftop. He casts a shadow as long as day.

I plan to ask Lupe's landlord if I can install skylights in her house. I'm thinking of putting one in the kitchen and one in the bathroom. Lupe would be able to grow herbs in the kitchen. When we're potty-training Destiny, she can sit in the bathroom and read children's books without straining her eyes. I can't imagine that the landlord will say no. The house will look prettier. We'll increase the property values. He'll have no clue as to my real motives. Lupe and I have seen more than our share of darkness, crossing borders under a waning moon and through starless nights. I want our lives to be flooded with light. Rings and rings of light, into eternity.

The Black Rebozo

Lupe and Marcos

Lupe sleeps. She dreams of a baby in a basket made of reeds. The basket is floating across the Rio Grande on gently lilting waters. Stars flicker overhead, illuminating a milky moon that looks like a breast. Lupe walks to the river's edge and steps in, walks until the water is knee high. The silt tugs at her feet, she feels her feet growing roots, anchoring her as she waits. She stretches her arms out in the direction of the basket.

She sings a song of praise to God: "*Bendito, bendito, bendito sea Dios. Los angeles cantan y alaban a Dios. Los angeles cantan y alaban a Dios.*" The baby in the basket is closer now; Lupe's song is pulling her in note by note. Lupe looks down at the water around her legs. The river is a mirror. When the child arrives Lupe will have her look into the water so that she can see her face for the first time. Lupe removes her black rebozo. She'll need it to wrap the baby in, to keep her warm for the walk back home. It's her mother's rebozo. It smells like roses, the roses that the pregnant Lady of Guadalupe gave the Indian, Juan Diego—in midwinter—so that he could prove to the bishop that she had indeed appeared.

Yes, this is the night for miracles, Lupe thinks. All she has to do is pray and wait—what she has done all her life—trusting in God's mercy. A breeze kicks up. For a moment Lupe loses sight of the basket and its treasure, but then she spots it again. It won't be long now, Lupe thinks. She dips her hand in the water and makes the sign of the cross.

A breeze kicks up again, turns to wind, to gusts that blow the stars out like birthday candles. The moon slips under a cloud. The gently undulating water begins to churn, to swirl. Lupe looks down toward her feet. The water is no longer clear; it has turned a muddy brown. The river is hungry, Lupe thinks, as she watches the water swallow floating branches of cottonwood and salt cedars. She pulls the blue corn meal from her pocket that she uses to make *atole*. She tosses a handful into the river. "*Mijita*," Lupe says, "come this way, follow my voice."

But the cornmeal isn't enough to calm the river. It is a snake now, in search of prey. It swallows the basket and the baby whole. "*Mijita*," Lupe cries out. "Where are you? Come this way." She throws more cornmeal into the river and waits. But it does no good. Her treasure, her child, is nowhere to be found. She wraps the rebozo around her shoulders. It smells as sweet as the breath of a newborn baby. Then Lupe understands. Her life as she knows it is over. Like La Llorona she will spend eternity haunting the river in search of her dead child.

"No!" Lupe shouts. "No!" until the sound of her own voice jolts her awake. Marcos sits up beside her, shakes her gently. "Lupita, you're having a nightmare. You're with me now. *Todo está bien.*"

"It was La Llorona, Marcos. The baby died, it was in a basket in the Rio Grande and"—Lupe sits up and presses her hand into the mattress. "Marcos, what's wrong? The mattress is wet." Marcos looks up at the ceiling. He hears the drumbeat of rain. "There must be a leak," he says, climbing out of bed.

Lupe pulls herself out of bed, too. Her nightgown around her thighs is soaked. She smiles. "There's a leak alright. My water broke. Our Destiny is on her way."

Moments later Lupe has her first contraction. She lets out a long, low moan. She feels like the earth is buckling beneath her, quaking. From now until the baby is born, there will be aftershocks.

"I'm getting you to the hospital now," Marcos says. *"Estoy preocupado.* Something might be wrong. The baby isn't due for another week. *Hay que hablar con el doctor."*

"Okay, okay, *pero calmate. No hay problema.* Just don't panic."

But Marcos is all panic. He is a man whose work requires that he measure everything before making a move: inches, feet, yards. Nothing has prepared him for the mysteries of women and water on a dark night. There is no math to explain how one woman, after nine months, breaks open and becomes two: mother and child.

Marcos draws the bedroom curtain open and looks outside. The rain is coming down hard, lightning shreds the sky. Dangerous road conditions, he thinks. He takes a deep breath. The man who cannot sleep without the closet light on summons all his courage. It's up to him to drive carefully, to deliver his beloved to the hospital, where experts can work their magic and coax the child out into the light of day.

"I'm ready," Lupe says. While Marcos was pondering the weather, Lupe had dried herself off and slipped on a sweat shirt and sweat pants. She put their toothbrushes and a change of clothes in a plastic shopping bag along with an outfit for the baby and pan dulce to snack on. The contractions continue. Her body is not her own anymore. The baby has taken over everything.

At the hospital, a nurse's aide takes Lupe and Marcos to the birthing room. It smells of lavender. Paintings of flowers hang on the wall: geraniums, petunias, hollyhocks. The walls are adobe colored, the lights dim. Beside a day bed is a rocking chair with a stuffed teddy bear on it. In the middle of the room is a hospital bed. The room is so quiet you can't even hear it breathe, Lupe thinks. Suddenly there is sound coming from a CD player: the chirping of birds and the whoosh of ocean waves. Lupe is delighted. What a perfect place for Destiny to be born, she thinks, it's so peaceful here, so cozy.

A nurse and midwife enter the room and greet the couple. They remind Marcos of doves cooing as they hover over Lupe, checking her pulse and blood pressure and other vital signs. "Very good, all is well," they coo. "But be prepared, it could be a very long day."

Marcos looks around the room again. He eyes the teddy bear. He wonders if he has watched too many *telenovelas*: when he thinks of birth he thinks of doctors in white masks and surgical gloves in a white, well-lit room. He thinks of trays beside the hospital bed with scalpels and forceps, and the chemical smell of disinfectant. In this room there's not even a burner for boiling water—although he has no idea what the water is used for, but that's how it's done on TV.

As if reading his mind, the nurse reassures him, "There are doctors close by on call if we need assistance." The midwife adds, "Don't worry. Women have been doing this since the beginning of time."

To help bring on labor, Lupe is told that she must walk. The midwife directs the couple to a hall off the waiting room. Marcos takes Lupe's hand and the two set out on their journey up and down the hall, the longest journey of their lives. Other women are walking, too. They look like goddesses, Lupe thinks, as they float by, their breasts and bellies engorged beneath floral gowns. Spanish, English, Vietnamese, Navajo: they laugh and moan and chatter in these languages, hallowing the hall, their voices echoing as if in a cathedral.

"You okay?" Lupe asks Marcos. "*Claro que sí*," he says, but it's not true. Marcos grasps the architecture of these goddess bodies. The women's babies have outgrown their rooms. They are straining against the walls of their mother's wombs, destabilizing the entire edifice. In El Salvador he knew of mothers dying while giving birth. He worries that something could happen to Lupe.

"*Y tú*, are you okay?" he asks Lupe. "Yeah," she says, but it's not true. For many months now her worries for her baby have run deep, grown roots like her potted geraniums. But they never blossomed: her fears were invisible to her friends. She believes it is bad luck to talk of worries about birth; the ripples of anxiety might engulf the child and harm her in some way. She remembers a neighbor in Mexico who went into labor. The baby died before being born. The woman's body, for nine months a cradle, turned into a coffin.

To make those thoughts go away, to pray for Destiny's safe arrival, Lupe whispers an Our Father. But she only gets half way through, *on earth as it is in heaven.* She feels God's absence as never before. Her prayer is a message slipped into a bottle and thrown into the ocean, adrift in a sea of unanswered prayers.

But the more they walk this hall of wails and chatter and laughter, the more hopeful they become. "Feel this," Lupe says. She places Marcos's hand at the bottom of her abdomen. "It feels like it might be the baby's head—or else her tummy," he says. They smile, relieved. The walking seems to be positioning the child. They sense that they are in the hands of a force that is perhaps greater than God: gravity. The tiny creature is preparing for a landing. Lupe thinks of a space shuttle returning to earth. Marcos thinks of the times he has jumped from the rung of a ladder, gravity always pulling him down, balanced, on his two feet.

"*Imagínate, Lupita, tú vas a dar luz,*" Marcos says. He prefers the Spanish phrase over the English for giving birth: *dar luz.* To give light, to bring forth light. Lupe starts to say something but instead she lets out a wail that she cannot muffle. Marcos grasps her shoulders, afraid she will collapse from the pain. "We're going to see the nurse right now," Marcos says.

Lupe grips her abdomen and takes a full breath, lets it out, smiles.

"Don't be silly, *mi amor.*" If you want to make me feel better, call up our friends. They're awake by now. I'm going to rest in the birthing room. I need to get my strength back. I'll ask the nurse if everyone can come in to say a quick hello. "*Donde 'sta tu cell phone?*" she asks. "*Lo tengo aquí,*" Marcos says, pulling it from his pocket. "I'll call right away."

❖

The friends march into the waiting room: Cory, Peter, Maritza, Flor.

"How's Lupe?" they ask, frantic. "She wasn't supposed to have the baby until next week," Cory says.

"Everything is normal," Marcos reassures them. "After Lupe rests, the nurse might let all of us go to the birthing room to say hello."

"Bet you never dreamed this would happen on your birthday, Marcos," Peter says. "Happy fortieth."

"Happy fortieth!" the others chime in. Peter nods at Flor. She pulls a package out of a large paper sack and hands it to Marcos. The gift is wrapped in the sports page from *The New York Times* and adorned with ribbons and bows.

"You didn't have to," Marcos said. But he's grinning, tearing up the sports page wrapping-paper like a child at Christmas. Then he freezes. In his hands is a box with a photo of a camera on it. "Open it, open it," Maritza says. Marcos opens the package, hands trembling. He removes a black Nikon camera and holds it in his cupped hands for several long moments. He lifts it up, amazed at its heft and grip. He runs his fingers around the lens as if searching for a pulse, as if the camera were a living thing. Then he removes the lens cap and holds the camera up to his eye. He looks through the viewfinder at a woman in a black rebozo, elated as she prepares to take her baby home. "We bought it used," Flor says, "but it's in perfect condition." "The manual," Cory adds," is in English and Spanish."

"*Gracias, gracias,*" Marcos says, his words sounding more like a prayer than a simple thank you. His face sparkles with tears. "Let's look at the manual," he says. "I want to learn how to—."

"Mr. Martinez!" A nurse's aide standing at the entry to the waiting room calls out to Marcos. "Come quickly." Marcos dashes after her to the birthing room, certain that something has gone wrong. But fear turns to shock, then wonder: Lupe is on the hospital bed, which is tilted slightly forward, her legs parted and covered with a sheet. The nurse and midwife hover over her, present at this mystery that has Lupe wailing and moaning, grunting and panting. "Lupe has reached full dilation," the midwife says. "It's time to push."

Marcos stands at Lupe's side, takes her hand, and kisses it. "*Te amo,* Lupita," he whispers. He wipes the film of sweat from Lupe's forehead. Then he joins the midwife in her chant: *breathe, push, breathe, push.*

"I can't do this anymore, *no puedo,*" Lupe says. She closes her eyes. Her body is on fire. "You can do it, Lupe," Marcos says. "I'm here with you, I'm breathing with you." Lupe's face is hot with tears but she manages a smile. She knows the baby's destiny is sealed: the girl has begun her pilgrimage out of the birth canal.

"Okay, come over here now, Mr. Martinez," the midwife says, "and watch your daughter being born."

Marcos is astonished by what he sees. Slowly, slowly the baby's head emerges from Lupe's body. Lupe groans. "She's almost here," the midwife tells her. "One more push." The midwife tells Marcos to place his hands near hers, by the baby's head. Lupe pushes. A moment later the rest of the baby's body slides out with a gush of liquid into the waiting hands of Marcos and the midwife.

Expelled from the paradise of her mother's womb, Destiny lets out her first cry. To Marcos's ears, she is a kitten, meowing. To

Lupe's ears, she is a bell, pealing. The nurse snips the umbilical cord, then has Marcos place the baby on her mother's chest.

"You made it, *mijita*," Lupe says, laughing and crying. "You made it over the border." Marcos kisses Destiny's tiny head. "*Gracias*, Lupita," he says. "You've given me the greatest gift I've ever had. I'll never forget this day, *nunca*."

Then he remembers. On the rocking chair, in the lap of the teddy bear, is his new camera. Marcos picks it up and returns to Lupe's side. He focuses the lens and snaps a picture of her and the baby. Then he zooms in and takes a picture of Lupe's left hand, which is resting on the baby's back. Lupe is wearing her wedding ring, silver with turquoise nuggets. She looks up at her husband. "We're all here now. *Aquí. Una familia.*" She kisses Destiny's forehead. "You did it, *preciosa*. You followed my voice."

◆

Dear Mama,

It's two in the morning and I'm here at my dorm room desk writing this letter by candlelight—a flame dancing inside a tall glass bearing the image of Our Lady of Guadalupe. I got the letters you sent me, Mama. This afternoon I put on a raincoat and boots and walked to the college mail room. I unlocked my box and pulled out a fat envelope with your return address. I ran all the way back to my dorm and tore open the envelope, hoping a word from you would help ease the loneliness I've felt since last week when I boarded the plane that tore me away from Albuquerque—away from you and Papa and my aunts and uncle, Maritza, Flor, Cory, and Peter.

I read each letter, astonished, my loneliness lightening with each word. I realized that, thanks to you, I have never been alone—not even when I was topsy-turvy and floating inside of you, a perfect stranger you befriended with a Big Chief tablet and a pen. We had adventures, didn't we Mama? You reading Harry Potter to me not only in English but in Spanish to "smarten me up." So here I am in Cambridge, Massachusetts of all places, *tu lengua preciosa, Español, mi pasaporte*: at the Latino Center I am making friends with people from all over the Spanish-speaking world, *palabra por palabra cruzando fronteras*, erecting bridges, bull-dozing walls.

"For posterity!" I can just imagine my aunts and uncle pleading with you to write letters—and they were right to do so because as you said, it would have been too easy to forget your stories. (It's bad enough a thief broke in and took the safe box with the other letters you wrote.) All this has me thinking about what I should do for my American History project. Our professor said we could write a paper, or create a work of art, or write poetry about some aspect of North American life. I'm thinking I would like to write a group of poems about you and Papa—what it was you fled from that brought you to the United States—this land of immigrants. You know what, Mama? I think that's exactly what I'll do, it's the perfect project. Because otherwise the history books will turn you and Papa and all the people like you into statistics, without faces, or voices. People without stories. Of course I'm talking as if my little poems could make a difference. But as you've shown me with your letters, better to err on the side of Posterity.

I know how you and Papa sacrificed so that I could go to college. I wanted to thank you by graduating with straight As, a pretty hopeless task I now see, surrounded as I am by students who graduated from prep schools, leaving me at least for this first year at a disadvantage. So your phone call on Monday came as an answer to my prayer when you told me out of the blue not to sweat it, that you would be as proud if I got nothing but Cs in my classes for the next four years, that Cs are nothing to sneeze at in this vale of tears, in these end times. So I will do my best, Mama. At the very least I will be fulfilling your dream for me: I cried when I read in one of the letters that you hoped someday I would be pushing a pen instead of a broom. Just remember Mama, you too pushed a pen: You pushed and pushed, writing letters to your Destiny, words that shimmer now in this pool of candlelight far from home.

As for the end times? I worry you will make yourself depressed, obsessing about the end times, although so far you seem to be doing pretty well, for all I know feeling a bit giddy that the Rapture is at hand. But I've been thinking. In spite of everything that is happening on the planet, it could well be that we are at the beginning times. Maybe if we work hard enough and believe enough, we will catch a glimpse of what this world might be

_____

like if we only loved it as it deserves to be loved. Things would change. Oh Lord, now I'm starting to sound like Aunt Flor!

Okay Mama, I'll close here. I want to read the letters one more time before I go to bed. I know your monthly block meeting will go well. Congratulations on the *Albuquerque Journal* story about the campaign you have kicked off, demanding of clothes manufacturers that they make women's clothing with pockets as they do with men's clothing. *¡Sigue adelante y hasta la victoria siempre!*

All my love to you,

Destiny

PS: You'll be happy to hear that the Block Captain's daughter carries her credit card in her bra, safe and sound!

Acknowledgments

I wish to thank the following:

Frank Zoretich, who took his red pen and bloodied up early drafts of stories.

The Lannan Foundation, which made it possible to spend a month in Marfa, Texas, where I could dream up the lives of my characters.

Sojourners Magazine, which first published "The Annunciation" (December 2008).

Above all, Susan Sherman, who believed in this project when I did not and offered editing help toward the end.

And, finally, many thanks to R.C. Davis-Undiano, friend, mentor, whose passionate love of Chicano literature has sustained so many writers in their work. We're profoundly grateful.